LACHLAN'S HEART

Book Two of the MacCulloughs

SUZAN TISDALE

Cover design by Wicked Smart Designs

Copyright © 2021 Suzan Tisdale

All rights reserved. No part of this publication may be reproduced, distributed, or transmitted in any form or by any means, including photocopying, recording, or other electronic or mechanical methods, without the prior written permission of the publisher, except in the case of brief quotations embodied in critical reviews and certain other noncommercial uses permitted by copyright law.

ISBN: 978-1-943244-97-3

Also by Suzan Tisdale

<u>The Clan MacDougall Series</u>

Laiden's Daughter

Findley's Lass

Wee William's Woman

McKenna's Honor

The Clan MacDougall Boxed Set

<u>The Clan Graham Series</u>

Rowan's Lady

Frederick's Queen

<u>The Mackintoshes and McLarens Series</u>

Ian's Rose

The Bowie Bride

Rodrick the Bold

Brogan's Promise

<u>The MacCulloughs</u>

Black Richard's Heart

Lachlan's Heart

<u>The Clan McDunnah Series</u>

A Murmur of Providence

A Whisper of Fate

A Breath of Promise

The Clan McDunnah Boxed Set

<u>Moirra's Heart Series</u>

Stealing Moirra's Heart

Saving Moirra's Heart

<u>Stand Alone Novels</u>

<u>Isle of the Blessed</u>

<u>Forever Her Champion</u>

<u>The Edge of Forever</u>

<u>In the Echo of a Kiss</u>

The MacAllens and Randalls Series:

Secrets of the Heart

The Daughters of Moirra Dundotter Series:

Mariote

Esa

Muriale

Orabilis

<u>The Brides of the Clan MacDougall</u>

(A Sweet Series)

Aishlinn

Maggy

Nora

For Kathryn Lynn Davis, Catherine Bybee, Bobbie Gordon, Chasity Bowlin, Hallee Bridgeman, and Terry Maggert. 2020 sucked rotten eggs, but you kept me sane. For that, I am eternally in your debt.

Prologue

Whores.

He hated whores above all other things.

Nasty, filthy, disgusting creatures, each and every one.

There were some people who were of the mistaken belief that a woman only became a whore out of sheer desperation. He knew that not to be the truth. 'Twas a lie told to justify their sinful ways. "Och! Feel sorry for me, for I have to spread my legs in order to survive!"

Lies. All lies.

He'd known the truth for years.

These so-called innocent women liked doing what they did. They enjoyed warming a man's bed, spreading their legs for a few bits of silver. How many times had he heard one whore or another, through thin walls, moaning and groaning with pleasure?

They mocked God, laughed in his face, ignoring his dictates and the laws of the church. And for what? A bit of coin and a few moments of wicked, sinful pleasure.

Aye, he knew the truth. With the fervent belief that God hated these women as much as he did, he also believed 'twas up to him to do God's work. No one else was going to.

The first kill had been the single most thrilling moment of his life, and one he liked to re-experience on occasion in the late night hours. Alone in his little room, he would relive that magical moment from a year ago when he'd realized his own truth and mission in life.

The sheer terror in her eyes had been beautiful. She knew, knew she was going to die, still she begged for mercy. Of course, he ignored her pleas; she was a whore after all.

When the blade of his dirk slid across the tender flesh of her neck, it elicited a near rapturous sensation that tickled up and down his spine. And when the blood gushed from the ragged, gaping wound? The sound of her gurgled last breaths? 'Twas bliss. Sheer, unadulterated bliss. He had taken her worthless life and sent her straight to hell where she belonged.

'Twas a righteous thing he did; 'twas God's work he was doing. Let no one say otherwise.

The second and third kills were almost as pleasurable, but lacked a certain something. Still, he kept on trying to recapture that thrilling sensation of the first. After sending his sixth whore to the bowels of hell, he decided it no longer mattered if the thrill was as intense as the first. Nay, 'twas God's work he was doing and that was all that mattered.

A whore is a whore is a whore. And God help him, he'd rid the world of these filthy vermin.

One whore at a time.

Chapter One

Love is, at the best of times, an odd business.

One moment, you're minding your own business and simply enjoying nothing more than a kinship with someone. It can go on like that for days, weeks, or-in Lachlan and Keevah's case-a few short months. Then the next thing you know, one of the parties falls hopelessly, head-over-heals in love with the other. If God is kind and benevolent, He sees to it that the second party feels much the same way as the first.

As it pertains to Lachlan and Keevah, they were simply two lonely people who enjoyed one another's company. Aye, *that* came as quite a surprise to each of them. Brought together unexpectedly during very troubled times, they fell into a quiet and amicable companionship that neither of them could have foreseen.

Keevah had come to live amongst the MacCulloughs more than five years ago. She kept herself to herself for a whole host of reasons. The primary one being she was a former prostitute from Inverness. Once that secret came to be known to the rest of the clan, she was given the moniker the *auld whore*. The name stuck to her like a burr and the clans people had avoided her like the plague ever since. That was five years ago.

Lachlan, however, was one of the few people who never once held her past against her. Most women, he reckoned, didn't choose to take up that line of work. Nay, 'twas almost always fate and circumstance, the fear of starvation or freezing to death, that forced women down that particular path.

He refused to pry. If she wanted to discuss the matter, she would. And if she didn't, well, 'twas neither here nor there. He enjoyed her company and that 'twas all that mattered. She was a good woman, her past be damned.

Had it not been for his cousin and laird's new bride, Aeschene, Lachlan doubted he and Keevah would ever have taken the time to get to know one another. Neither of them questioned their newfound friendship. They simply appreciated having someone to talk to.

So, as it happened, the friendship formed quickly.

But then one chilly, yet bright autumn day, Lachlan woke and realized, to his own utter astonishment, that he was quite hopelessly in love with one Keevah MacElroy.

It shocked him to his marrow.

He reckoned he could spend the next few years trying to figure out how it had happened. But no amount of studying the matter would change anything. He was in love. And that, as they say, was that. 'Twas best to take a thing head on and deal with it, like any good warrior.

Aye, Keevah was a breathtakingly beautiful young woman with a smile that could light up the darkest of nights. But Lachlan was attracted to her on a much deeper level. He didn't know all her secrets, for those weren't nearly as important as her character. The woman possessed a giving heart, a genuineness of spirit, and a streak of independence he sincerely admired. What was it his grandfather used to say? *Beauty fades but a warm heart will last forever.* Aye, 'twas the beauty of her soul that mattered most.

The only problem he now faced was how he was going to tell her and what would she think of it all?

Chapter Two

'Twas only a few days ago that Lachlan realized how deeply he loved the beautiful Keevah MacElroy. However, there hadn't been enough time to let her in on his newfound discovery.

There was the rescue of Richard, Rory, and Colyne to be dealt with, then the subsequent attack against their mortal enemies the Chisolms - within the MacCullough keep, mind you.

Then there was the business of hanging Randall Chisolm that had to be tended to.

And if those weren't adequate distractions enough, he was forced to watch while his best friend Rory married the comely Marisse MacRay; Aeschene's maid and friend. He kept his jealousy to himself and congratulated the newly wedded couple.

Just when he thought he could take a deep breath and seek out Keevah, Richard requested his presence to *discuss a verra important matter.*

The *verra important matter* revolved around their newly gotten gains. It turned out that while Lachlan and other MacCullough warriors - along with a few hundred MacDougall men - had been fighting against the band of Chisolms assembled here, Black Richard

MacCullough's longtime friend and ally, Caelen McDunnah was wrenching the Chisolm keep out of the hands of those Randall warriors he had left behind to guard it.

That had been the man's second biggest mistake in the past few weeks. His first was underestimating Aeschene MacRay and her determination to rescue her husband from his evil clutches. Both poor decisions had led to his death.

And the world was a much better place without Randall Chisolm in it.

'Twas no small task, no small task indeed that Richard and Aeschene were asking of him. They wanted Lachlan to act as interim chief and laird of the Chisolm keep and all its holdings. 'Twas a temporary position, if one could call twenty years or so *temporary*. "Just until our first born is old enough to take over the helm," Richard had explained.

Aeschene had thought to entice him with the promise of gold. Had it been anyone else insulting him thusly, he would have gutted them. But it was Aeschene, a lovely woman with a heart the size of Scotia. 'Twas her only saving grace; that and the fact she not only *willingly* married his cousin, Black Richard MacCullough, she had also found him in possession of redeeming qualities others weren't able to see. She loved the man. He certainly hoped Richard knew just how lucky he truly was.

Now he found himself atop the parapet looking out at the only place he'd ever called home. The sun was just beginning to creep up over the horizon, a splash of blood-red against the indigo blue sky. He loved this time of day; the last few lingering moments of night, with stars that still twinkled before being outshined by the morning sun.

He'd be taking a handful of MacCullough warriors with him on this new journey, as well as nearly one hundred MacDougalls. Thankfully, the MacDougall laird and chief, Angus, had volunteered his fine warriors to help to ensure a smooth transition of leadership.

Lachlan knew it wasn't going to be easy gaining the fealty of the Chisolms and harder still to get them to willingly take the MacCullough name. Therefore, he and Richard were quite glad for Angus's offer.

Not once in all his years had he wished to be chief or laird of any clan. Truly, the thought never entered his mind.

Now, in the course of a day, he'd been given the rarest of opportunities to be and do just that. 'Twas an honor to even be considered for such a great and noble endeavor. Aye, it was also a significant responsibility. He'd not shirk his duty and he'd make damned certain that when it came time for Richard and Aeschene's first born to claim their birthright, they'd not be disappointed.

He could think of no one better to help him in this pursuit than Keevah. With her by his side, there was naught he couldn't do, no mission he couldn't accomplish, no mountain he could not climb. He'd be invincible; unstoppable.

Now if only he could convince her of that.

THE MORNING WAS NOT GOING AS HE HAD PLANNED. HE HAD HOPED to avoid any prolonged goodbyes between himself his cousins. Saying goodbye to Richard, Raibeart and Colyne had been difficult, but not nearly as difficult as with Aeschene. The poor woman had cried so much that Richard ordered her back to bed. "Ye are the brother I always wanted," she told him through hiccups. Considering she had four brothers by blood and two by law, he found that an exceedingly odd statement. But given that she was heavy with child, he decided not to point out what he considered to be rather obvious. In truth, he was going to miss the feisty woman. He was also going to miss Raibeart and Colyne more than he cared to admit. With Aeschene's love and guidance, the boys had given up their heathen ways. If that wasn't a miracle, he didn't know what was.

It had taken more than an hour for those dreaded goodbyes to the only family he'd known since he was a child.

At Richard's behest, he also stopped to tell Angus McKenna and Duncan McEwan thank you. The two men and their army of fine warriors had been instrumental in the battle against the Chisolms. Had it not been for them, Lachlan knew 'twould be he and the rest of his family still hanging from the gallows and not Randall Chisolm.

What was meant to be a quick *thank ye for your help* ended up being an hour-long discussion regarding Lachlan's future and what was the best way to win the Chisolms over. Angus felt a more diplomatic approach would serve him well. Duncan, however, was of the mindset that Lachlan should simply banish or kill anyone who refused to give him their fealty.

In the end, he promised to take both their opinions under advisement. Satisfied, the two men promised that should he ever need them in the future, all he need do is send word. For that he would be forever grateful.

As he made his way through the courtyard, one person after another felt it necessary to offer their best wishes and fond farewells. At this rate, it would be a week before they reached their new holding.

Most of the men he was taking with him were assembled near the gate, readying horses and supplies for the journey. Believing everything was under control, he decided to leave them to their work while he went to see Keevah. Yet every time he began to make his way towards the woman's cottage, someone would call out his name, needing his help with one thing or another. He was getting his first glimpse at what being the chief of a clan would look like. Thus far, he was unimpressed.

They should have left hours ago. He'd moved past frustrated and straight into furious with the constant questions and delays.

Annoyed, he pulled young Jamie MacCullough aside. "I am declaring ye my second in command," Lachlan told him. Jamie's wide-eyed expression said he firmly believed Lachlan had lost his mind. "Me?"

"Aye, ye," he declared as he began walking away. Jamie was a good lad, at least ten years his junior. While he was quite skilled with sword and mace and possessed a good head on his shoulders, those weren't the reasons he'd chosen him. He was simply the closest man available.

"Jamie MacCullough is my second in command!" Lachlan called out to anyone within shouting distance. Those still packing supplies onto horses glanced up, shrugged their shoulders, then immediately went back to work. Without waiting for questions or comments, he spun on his heel and headed toward Keevah's cottage.

His carefully prepared speech evaporated from his mind

completely the moment she opened the door. She stole his very breath away.

Raven black hair that was nearly blue when the sunlight hit it just so, was carefully braided and draped over one shoulder, where it cascaded almost to her waist. Gloriously thick hair that framed what he felt was the most perfect oval-shaped face. Full, pink lips that he was quite certain would feel as soft as rose petals, formed a smile that didn't quite reach her eyes.

"Ye have heard?" he asked from the doorway.

A curt nod was her only reply before she turned away. Ducking his head low, he stepped inside. Her cottage was immaculate, not just neat and tidy. A brazier stood in the center of the small space with two small stools on opposite sides. A small bed tucked against the opposite wall, a small kitchen with a window that let in the early morning light. Her loom sat on the south wall, under a slightly larger window.

Like him, she appreciated order in her life. Just like him, she couldn't stand chaos. There wasn't a thing out of place, save for her half-smile and silence. Mayhap this was a sign that she was going to miss him as much as he was going to miss her.

"I wish I had more time to discuss this with ye, Keevah," he said as he gently closed the door.

"What is there to discuss?" she said with a shrug of indifference. "'Tis a great honor they have bestowed upon ye. Ye will make a fine chief, Lachlan."

Patiently, he waited in silence in the quiet hope that she would eventually turn around and look at him. Preferably soon.

"Keevah, I will be back in a fortnight," he said, his tone encouraging. "I want ye to wait for me."

When she turned to look at him there was no doubt she was puzzled. "Wait for ye?"

"Aye," he said, taking a cautious step toward her.

"To what end?" she asked as she tilted her head to one side.

He offered her his most sincere smile. More than anything, he wanted to give her the words of his heart. He could hear one of his men calling for him as he came down the path.

"Keevah, I want ye to ken that I sincerely value the friendship that has sprouted betwixt us these past weeks," he said in a soft, warm voice. "Ye made the most difficult times far more tolerable."

He watched as she wrapped her arms around her waist. She said nothing and kept her back to him. Whoever was calling his name was growing nearer. Damn! He wished he had more time.

"I am glad for yer friendship as well, Lachlan," she said. Her voice was nothing but a whisper, giving him a glimmer of hope. *If the leavin' is difficult, mayhap it is because she has the same feelin's for ye.*

"Keevah, will ye please look at me?"

There was a knock at the door – one of his men calling out his name. "Lachlan, Jamie says we must go," came a voice from the other side.

She took in a deep breath before turning around. "Ye must nae tarry," she said, giving a slight nod toward the door. "I wish ye well, Lachlan."

Another knock, louder this time. "Lachlan! Are ye in there?"

"Keevah-" He was interrupted by another loud knock.

Frustrated, he yanked open the door. "Tell Jamie and the others to wait," he ordered. "And dinnae bother me again."

Properly chastised, the young man spun on his heels and left as if his toes were on fire. Satisfied, Lachlan shut the door and turned back to Keevah.

"Ye should nae make yer men wait," she told him.

He chuckled softly. "They will nae leave without me."

He was, after all, their new chief and laird. While he knew he had a duty and responsibility to his men, there was a more important duty standing before him.

"I want ye to marry me."

She spun on her heel; her eyes grew as big and round as wagon wheels. "What?"

"I want to marry ye," he repeated.

"But why?" she asked incredulously.

Chuckling again, he took a step forward. "Because I love ye, Keevah."

THE SINCERITY IN HIS VOICE, THE GENUINE LOOK OF ADORATION IN his big brown eyes was unmistakable. Her heart cracked with the knowledge that she could never be his wife. The last thing she'd ever want to do was bring him even a moment of pain. While she had recently come to the realization that she cared for him, far more than she felt she had a right to, there was no possible way she could agree to be his wife. No matter how badly she wanted to.

"Ye need a better, finer woman than me," she said.

"I can think of nae better woman to take as my wife than ye, Keevah."

She knew him well enough to know that he wouldn't go down without a fight. Once he made his mind up about something, there was very little chance of getting him to change it. "I am the auld whore, remember?"

A flash of fury erupted behind his dark eyes. "Never say that again," he told her through gritted teeth. "That was yer past, nae who ye are now. I dunnae care about what ye once were."

"But ye should care," she told him, her tone biting.

"Keevah, ye could nae help what happened to ye. Many women are forced into that kind of life through no fault of their own."

She openly scoffed at him, knowing he was trying to be noble and kind. But he didn't know the truth. "Ye do nae ken me or why I did what I did. Ye will never understand."

From his furrowed brow and slitted eyes, she could tell that wasn't the answer he had expected.

There were many reasons why she'd chosen to take that particular path in her life. No one, not even Lachlan, would ever be able to understand.

He was silent for a long moment. "I dunnae care about the why of it, Keevah. I only ken that I love ye and want ye for my wife."

She swallowed hard, wishing he would hurry up and leave so that she could spend the rest of her life grieving the loss of his friendship and all that *might* have been. "And what would ye do the first time a man smiles at me? Will ye be wonderin' if he is a man from my past? And what if he were?"

A tic was beginning to form in his square jaw. She could tell he hadn't given that any thought.

Lord above, she didn't want to hurt him. She didn't want them to part on bad terms. "Go, Lachlan," she murmured.

"I will nae go unless I have yer promise that ye will at least think about my proposal," he said. With his arms crossed over his chest, she knew he wasn't about to budge without making the promise.

Swallowing hard, she acquiesced, knowing full well she could think about it until the end of time and her answer would never change. "Aye, I will think about it." 'Twould be impossible for her to think of anything else.

Satisfied, he smiled, looking much relieved with her answer. "I love ye, Keevah. I will be back in a fortnight. Three weeks at most."

She waited until the door closed behind him before she let the tears fall. Aye, she loved him far more than she ought, but she knew a man like Lachlan MacCullough deserved a better woman than she.

But knowing that hard truth didn't make the leaving any easier.

AS HE CLOSED THE DOOR BEHIND HIM, LACHLAN COULDN'T ESCAPE the sensation that he was leaving one life behind in pursuit of another. It damned near cleaved his heart in twain to leave her. He wanted nothing more than to go back inside, toss her over his shoulder, and drag her away, to start their future together now. Resisting that urge, he turned and walked away. He couldn't and wouldn't force her into anything. She would have to come to him willingly or not at all.

While she had made the promise to think about his proposal, deep down he knew her answer would be the same the next time he asked.

Slowly, he made his way along the path and made a silent promise to himself. *Upon my return, I will somehow convince her to marry me. I will make her see the rightness of our union.*

I will win her heart if it is the last thing I do.

Without looking back, he made his way to his waiting men. Taking to his horse, he gave the call to head out.

Ahead, the unknown. Behind him, the only woman he could ever love.

⁓⸱⸱⸱⸱⸱⁓

From the little window near her door, Keevah wept as she watched Lachlan walk away.

No matter how much she genuinely wanted to be his wife, she knew that was not her future, nor his. Now that he would be interim chief of a clan, he needed a woman whose past would not come back to haunt either of them. A woman without all her secrets; secrets that could potentially ruin many lives. Secrets she could never reveal to anyone. Secrets she must take to her grave.

She firmly believed that a marriage, any marriage, should be based on a foundation of sincerity and honesty. Nay, Lachlan was a good man and he deserved both those things and more. And honesty, divulging long buried secrets, was not something she could give to him. Every-thing else, love, adoration, respect, aye, those things she could give. But if she were not completely honest, then all those things she could give him would be tainted.

She hadn't been allowed to spend the remainder of her day awash in heartache. Less than an hour after Lachlan departed, one of the kitchen maids was knocking at her door.

"Aeschene has sent for ye," the girl said.

Keevah took note of the young woman's profoundly red cheeks. *See? This is all the proof ye need to ken ye've made the right decision. If a kitchen maid cannae speak to ye without shame or embarrassment, then how could ye possibly expect to be a laird's wife? Nay, ye'd bring naught more than over-whelming embarrassment to yer husband.*

Keevah told the brown-haired lass that she would be along directly. The poor girl scurried away, fearful, Keevah assumed, that if she tarried too long at her door, her tainted reputation might somehow rub off on her.

After washing her face, she grabbed her cloak, painted on a look of indifference, and headed out to see what Aeschene needed. All the while, with her heart breaking with each beat, she pretended that all was right in her world.

⁓⋅⋯✦⋯⋅⁓

Keevah's feigned indifference evaporated the moment she saw Aeschene. Her friend was in the gathering room, sitting next to the fire, a soft blanket draped across her knees. There were two things that brought forth her tears. Seeing the look of sheer contentment on Aeschene's face, and her burgeoning belly. In three months, Aeschene would be holding her first bairn in her arms, nursing him or her at her breast.

Contentment, motherhood, and knowing that above stairs a man who loved Aeschene more than his own life were symbols of all the things Keevah would never have.

Until Lachlan's proposal that morning, Keevah had resigned herself to knowing she'd never experience any of those beautiful moments in life. For years, she'd convinced herself she was happy and content.

But her heart, her shattering heart, finally spoke the truth and it was all too much. She ran to Aeschene and collapsed at her feet.

"Keevah? Is that ye?" Aeschene asked as she reached out to pat her head. The poor woman was very nearly completely blind. Keevah hadn't announced herself when she ran to her.

She nodded her head and sobbed an 'aye'.

"What on earth is the matter?" Aeschene asked, her voice tinged with a blend of confusion as well as concern.

Through tears and occasional sobs, Keevah described her earlier interaction with Lachlan, and his proposal.

"Och! Why would ye be cryin', Keevah? That is wonderful news."

"Nay," Keevah said, choking on a sob. "I cannae marry him."

"Do ye nae love him?"

"'Tis the God's truth I do," she said as she wiped her tears away with her fingertips. "More than anything, I love him."

"Then why can ye nae marry him?"

Had the woman forgotten everything she knew about Keevah?

"Ye ken why, Aeschene. Lachlan deserves much more than an auld whore as his wife."

Aeschene dismissed her argument in its entirety. "Bah! If Lachlan does nae care then why should ye?"

Keevah swallowed hard before answering. "Because what if some day we come across a man from my past? I dunnae want to be married to someone who might constantly be thinkin' *did my wife warm his bed?*"

"I doubt very seriously that Lachlan would ever think such a thing."

"But he *might*. And do ye nae think the Chisolms would nae be as forgivin' as ye?" She shook her head and closed her eyes tightly. "Nay, Aeschene, I dunnae want to bring any shame to Lachlan. And I dunnae want him to constantly be defendin' my honor."

Aeschene reached out and placed a warm palm on Keevah's cheek. "I think 'twould only take him needin' to do that once and the need would never arise again."

While she appreciated Aeschene's positivity and loyalty, she thought both were ill conceived and ill placed. She simply couldn't understand for she hadn't lived the kind of life Keevah had.

"Come now, and dry yer tears," Aeschene said as she withdrew a bit of linen from the sleeve of her blue dress and handed it to her.

"Now, I ken ye cannae see the suitability of marryin' Lachlan-"

"I cannae see the rightness of marryin' *any* man," Keevah interjected.

"Be that as it may," Aeschene said, ignoring her altogether. "Ye be a fine woman, Keevah. I may be blind, but even I can see the excellence of marryin' Lachlan. Ye would make him a good wife, of that, I have no doubt."

When Keevah began to argue otherwise; Aeschene would hear none of it. "Tell me, Keevah. How long do ye plan on punishin' yerself for the decisions ye made in the past?"

"I am nae-"

"Aye, ye *are*. Ye are punishin' yerself for yer past and refuse to think about yer future. A future that could be filled with so much love and happiness that it might seem too unbelievable."

"Aeschene, I ken ye're tryin' to help-"

Aeschene clicked her tongue and shook her head. "Then ye be lyin' when ye say ye love him more than anythin'."

Appalled at the accusation, Keevah sat as straight as an arrow. "But I *do* love him!"

"Nay. If ye truly loved him, and if ye truly valued yer friendship with him, ye would have said 'aye', and ye would be standin' before the priest. Ye would become his wife and partner. Instead, ye hide yer head in shame, punishin' yerself for yer past. Ye have sent Lachlan to live out the rest of his days alone as he tries to get the Chisolms under control and prepare a future for my child."

Her words hurt but didn't make them any less true. Keevah hadn't thought of it in those terms. "But he will find a wife. A better woman than I," she tried to argue.

"Nay," Aeschene said firmly. "If I ken anythin' at all about Lachlan, he will never marry. He will spend all the rest of his days waitin' for ye."

The thought of Lachlan living the rest of his life without anyone to love or be loved by, felt like a kick to her stomach.

"Will ye at least consider what I have said?" Aeschene asked with a raised brow.

Keevah swallowed back more tears. "I can assure ye, I will think of naught else."

WITH THE PROMISE MADE, AESCHENE MOVED THE DISCUSSION TO the reason she had sent for Keevah in the first place. "Now that Marisse is married, she will nae longer have the time to help me." Marisse had been her constant companion for several years; Aeschene's eyes to the rest of the world.

Keevah took the chair opposite her friend, soaking up the warmth from the hearth. She was only half listening, for her mind was still on Lachlan.

"I need someone to be my eyes, Keevah. Someone I can trust. Someone I can confide in."

"Have ye chosen that someone yet?"

Aeschene smiled. "Aye, I have. I would like *ye* to do it."

"Me?" Keevah was beyond surprised.

"And I swear, if ye tell me ye are nae good enough, or that yer past would somehow keep ye from sayin' 'aye', I will have to beat the bloody hell out of ye."

Keevah's eyes grew as wide as trenchers. She tried to find a good retort, but came up empty handed.

"I need ye, Keevah. I truly do. Next to Marisse, I consider ye my dearest friend."

It had been years since anyone had held her in such high esteem; since anyone considered her their dearest friend. A pang of ... longing perhaps, tugged at her already heavy heart. Kiernan. It had been more than five years since last she'd seen the young woman who'd been as close to her as a sister. But there wasn't a day that went by when she did not think of her. Not only was she a sister of her heart, but she was also the keeper of Keevah's secrets.

Aeschene's voice broke through her quiet reverie. "Will ye please do this for me?"

Keevah knew 'twould be as difficult to agree as it would be to decline. Saying yes meant she would have to watch every day as Aeschene's family grew. She'd be witness to the love shared between she and Black Richard. Both constant reminders of what she could never have.

But to say no, would mean she'd be turning her back on the friendship they had forged. She would go back to her little cottage and spend every day of the rest of her life alone. Suddenly, the thought of being truly alone no longer held the same appeal it once did.

"Aye, I will do this for ye."

Chapter Three

Three long days and nights of traveling in the cold, bitter rain, in mud up to their horses's knees, Lachlan and his men finally reached the Chisolm holding. Cold, filthy, and hungry, Lachlan wanted nothing more than a warm meal, a hot bath and fresh clothing, and to begin his life as laird.

Jamie, who took his position as second in command quite seriously, rode to his left. Determined to impress his new laird, Jamie worked twice as hard as anyone else in their army of one hundred sixty warriors.

To his right rode Fergus MacDougall, one of the men lent to him by Angus. Fergus was tall and lanky, mayhap no older than five and twenty, with ginger colored hair and dark blue eyes. Lachlan liked the young man for two important reasons. Firstly, he didn't speak unless he had something important to say. Secondly, he had been highly recommended by both Angus and Duncan. Apparently, he was a brilliant strategist. And according to Angus, the lad *is the pure definition of grace when it comes to a sword.*

They had just crested a large, wide hill when the keep first came into view. Jamie let out a low whistle as his eyes grew wide in wonder. Even Fergus was impressed, for he grunted approvingly.

Lachlan stared out in the same wide-eyed wonder. His first thought was that Keevah would have been just as awestruck as he and she would have found much beauty in this place. Where it pertained to first thoughts and Keevah, the two were inseparable. 'Twas impossible for him to have one without the other.

The main keep was four stories tall, with four square towers on each corner. Those towers were six stories tall.

Made of dark gray stone, the keep nestled into a grassy outcropping, surrounded on three sides by the largest loch he'd ever seen. That loch stretched on for as far as the eye could see. The early morning sun glinted against the blue-green water, making it sparkle and glimmer.

Surrounding the entire keep was a massive, well-fortified, crenelated stone wall some two stories in height. Just beyond the first wall was a wide courtyard and another equally fortified second wall, complete with a second set of gates that led into the bailey.

From his vantage point, he could see the large stables, a granary, and various other outbuildings. Dotted along the banks of the loch were numerous cottages.

To the east was a massive forest. This morning, the land was painted in a thousand shades of green.

The MacCullough keep could have fit into the bailey with room to spare. He'd never seen the like of it before.

He couldn't believe his cousin trusted this treasure to him. A momentary sensation of dread tugged at his insides. Lord, how he wished Keevah was here to help wipe away the doubts creeping into his mind.

"I have never seen the like of it before," Jamie whispered in a near reverent tone. "I doubt Edinburgh castle is that large."

Lachlan chuckled. "Nae, Edinburgh Castle is larger," he assured him. He'd seen it once, years ago when he was a lad. Before his father died, he'd taken him along with him on that journey. 'Twas one of the many fond memories he had of his father.

"Close yer mouth, Jamie," he said with a smile. "Lest the Chisolms think we are ill-bred and uneducated."

With a twinkle in his eye, Jamie said, "But we *are* ill-bred and uneducated."

"Aye, but they need nae ken that just yet."

THE INFAMOUS FIONA MACPHERSON MET LACHLAN AND HIS MEN just inside the first gate. There was no mistaking who she was. 'Twas the first time Lachlan had ever seen a woman in chainmail and armed to the teeth. Aside from that, she was just as beautiful as Richard had described.

"Lachlan MacCullough?" she called out as the men approached. Lined up behind her were at least two dozen McDunnah warriors. They too, were dressed for battle and well armed. The sight made the hair on the back of his neck stand on end.

"I am he," Lachlan replied as he steered his horse toward her. Dismounting, he gave her a slight bow from the waist.

"I am Fiona McPherson-McDunnah," she said - as if the woman needed any introduction.

"Ye seem prepared to do battle," he said with a raised brow and nod towards all the armor and weaponry. "Are we at war?"

"Aye, I fear we are, MacCullough."

MacCullough. It was going to take him a long while to get used to being referred to in that manner. "With what clan?"

A small band of young lads came to retrieve their horses. "Jamie, ye and Fergus are with me. Have the rest of the men tend to their horses, then get something to eat."

Jamie gave the order then hurried to catch up to his laird and Fiona.

"Not clan, but *clans*," she said as she began leading him toward the second wall in hurried fashion. Jamie and Fergus fell into step behind their laird. The McDunnah warriors followed alongside them.

Good lord! He'd only just arrived and now he must prepare for war with not one clan, but two. Mayhap more. "The Farquars?" They were more of a nuisance than any great threat, but they were the first clan that came to his mind.

Fiona laughed. "Nay," she said. "They ran like frightened rabbits when they saw us coming a week ago."

The gates pulled open as they approached and the large group spilled out into the bailey. Save for the warriors and a few scraggly looking dogs, the space was empty.

The keep was even more impressive up close and for the first time since he was a lad, he felt rather small.

"Then who?" he asked as they splashed through puddles heading toward the stairs.

"The MacGregors for one," she said.

The MacGregors. "They have been life-long allies to the Chisolms," he said. "One of my and Richard's biggest concerns were how they'd respond."

"Caelen believes they're simply worried over their future. With ye, us, and the MacDougalls, they are probably shittin' their trews worried we will try to take their lands."

'Twas a shock to hear a woman speak in such a manner. But then, Fiona MacPherson was not a typical woman. She said not another word as she led the group up the steps and into the massive keep.

FIONA LED THE WAY DOWN A LONG CORRIDOR AND THROUGH A SET of tall double doors. Within was one of the largest, grandest gathering halls he'd ever seen. *I have fought on smaller battlefields*, he mused as he took in the enormous space.

Large stone fireplaces lined the walls to his left and right. Overhead were six, heavy black iron chandeliers with dozens of candles blazing in each. A long, wooden high table, lined with benches sat on a dais in front of the fireplace on the eastern side of the room. Over the mantle hung the MacCullough banner. It appeared to have been torn in several spots and mended back together. It angered him to think someone would have torn it thusly, but he was thankful to whomever mended it.

Caelen McDunnah sat at that high table in the only chair. War braids lined both sides of his scarred face. 'Twas difficult to tell if he was amused or perturbed; both expressions were often similar. Two men were leaning in, speaking to him in hushed tones. Neither man looked pleased.

As Lachlan and the others approached, their heavy footfalls echoed off the walls and arched ceiling, drawing Caelen's attention away from the two men who were speaking to him. As soon as the man saw his beautiful wife, he smiled. Or leered. 'Twas difficult for Lachlan to tell. Either way, he did appear quite pleased at seeing his wife.

Now, Caelen McDunnah was legendary. He was known to start a fight simply because he enjoyed fighting. Ruthless and unforgiving on the field of battle, it was widely accepted throughout Scotland that Caelen McDunnah was the meanest, most relentless and ferocious son of a whore that ever walked God's earth. He was a terrifying man.

His wife, however, was not of that same mindset as the rest of the world. She bounded up the steps as he pushed himself away from the table. Lachlan watched as the two people shared a warm embrace. The public display of warmth and mutual admiration went against everything Lachlan thought he knew about the either of them. Love, he reckoned, could change a person. Thankfully, it hadn't softened Caelen's fighting abilities.

Caelen finally turned his attention toward Lachlan. "Ye look like death warmed over," he said by way of how-do-you-do.

Lachlan shrugged his shoulders. "It has been a long five years."

They grabbed each other's forearms in greeting. "How long has it been since last we've met?" Caelen asked.

"At least eight years," Lachlan said.

Caelen nodded, stepped aside, and pointed to the ornately carved chair. "'Tis yer seat now, MacCullough."

My seat.

Reluctantly, he stood behind the chair. This was the seat of power, so to speak. How many generations of lying, cheating, conniving Chisolms had sat in this very chair? Too many to count.

With one hand, Lachlan picked up the chair and called Jamie forward. "I am a MacCullough," he declared loudly. "I will nae defile the skin of my own arse by sittin' in that. The Chisolm clan is no more."

Uncertain just what he was meant to do with the former seat of power, Jamie gave a slight shrug of his shoulders and carried the thing out of doors.

Caelen chuckled loudly before giving Lachlan a firm slap on his back. The blow came close to knocking the air out of his lungs, but he wasn't about to let anyone know that.

"I like ye, MacCullough. Ye have bollacks, that's for certain."

Forgoing the formalities of the dais, the two men stepped to the hearth. Caelen waited for his wife to sit before taking the seat beside her. Lachlan sat opposite them.

"Richard sends his thanks and regards," Lachlan said.

"How are his brothers?" Fiona asked.

"They fair well." While Raibeart and Richard were healing nicely and would make a full recovery, Lachlan worried over Colyne. The young lad had been through hell and back. God only knew if there would be long suffering effects of his imprisonment. He kept those thoughts to himself for a wide variety of reasons. Mostly because that was a private family matter. And God only knew how riddled with ears the walls of this keep were.

"Fiona tells me we are at war," Lachlan said, wanting to get to the heart of the matter. The sooner he dealt with whatever problems there were, the better off he and his men would be. And he could get to the business of taking over.

"Aye," Caelen said as he scratched his stubbled jaw. "Ye be at war, all right. On two fronts."

"Fiona mentioned the MacGregors," Lachlan began before being interrupted by a serving maid bringing refreshments. A pretty lass of no more than four and ten he assumed, with fiery red hair, bright blue eyes, and freckles that dotted her nose. She carried a tray with three mugs. Caelen and Fiona declined, but Lachlan happily took a mug of ale from her tray.

"Ye might want to have someone taste that first," Caelen warned.

He paused, the mug a mere inch from his lips. "Ye jest."

"Nay, I dunnae jest."

The serving girl looked nervous; her eyes darting back and forth between Caelen and Lachlan.

"Meet yer new laird," Caelen told the frightened girl. "And take a sip of that ale in his honor."

She was horrified; tears began to fill her eyes. She'd been caught and knew it. Without uttering a sound, she fled from the gathering room.

Fiona carefully took the ale from Lachlan and poured the contents into the hearth. The flames sizzled as a cloud of smoke and steam rose up.

"I would nae eat or drink anything I did nae prepare myself," Caelen warned Lachlan. "Else ye will find pissed-filled ale, shite filled meat pies, or worse yet, poison."

Lachlan sat in stunned incredulity.

"I take it they have nae been too keen on havin' ye here," Lachlan said.

Caelen grunted as he shook his head. "That, lad, would be a monumental understatement. Thus far, we have put down three insurrections, a mutiny, and have tossed more Chisolms into their own dungeon than I can count."

Lachlan had been prepared for *some* troubles in the beginning, but this? Poison? Insurrection? All of that in a week's time?

Nay, he hadn't prepared himself for those things. However, he felt that with the right leadership, he could get the Chisolms to come around.

"I warn ye, MacCullough, the road ahead of ye will be rife with deceit and outright hostility. Apparently, their former lairds were all *loved beyond measure*, to hear them tell it."

Fiona gave a quick nod. "Aye, ye cannae find anyone who will say a bad word about Maitland or Randall Chisolm. They were *adored*."

"I dunnae give a damn about adoration. I care about fealty and honor," Lachlan told them. "I will nae settle for anything less."

Caelen leaned back in his chair, stretching his legs out towards the warm fire. "Dunnae say I didn't warn ye."

As long as he had the MacDougalls and MacCullough men alongside him, Lachlan firmly believed he could quash any further troubles from these people. "And I thank ye for the warnin'," he said. "Now, besides the MacGregors, who else are we at war with?"

Caelen threw his head back and laughed. "Lad, have ye nae been listenin'? Ye are still at war with the Chisolms."

"THUS FAR, IN THE FIVE DAYS WE HAVE BEEN HERE, WE HAVE PUT down three insurrections, two attempts to challenge the chiefdom, and detained five individuals who attempted to kill us through poison, arrows, and or a dirk to our heart," Caelen explained. "We have put so many people in the dungeon that it cannae take another. We have had to resort to keeping at least a dozen people locked in rooms above stairs."

Lachlan knew the transition of power wasn't going to be easy. But this news was beyond what he had anticipated. It was abundantly clear that the Chisolms were adamantly opposed to the idea of the MacCulloughs ruling over them.

"How many Chisolms have come to our side?" Lachlan asked, afraid he wasn't going to like the answer.

Caelen chuckled and shook his head. "None."

None? "I ken that should nae surprise me ..." Lachlan let out a frustrated breath.

"It surprises the hell out of me," Caelen said. "One would think that at least a handful of people would see the rightness in givin' ye their fealty," Caelen said.

"Until these past few days, I never thought I would meet anyone more stubborn that a McDunnah," Fiona began, "but I have been proven wrong more times than I care to admit."

Caelen laughed at his wife's blunt honesty.

"Were it yer clan now in charge, what course of action would ye be takin' to gain the fealty of these people?" Lachlan asked. He had a few ideas of his own, but he was ever open to listening to the wisdom of others.

"I'd have hung every last one of them," Caelen admitted. "Save for the women and children, but even *they* cannae be trusted at this point."

To Lachlan's surprise, Fiona readily agreed. "While I do like the notion of hanging the bloody bastards, doin' so would nae do anything but make them hate the MacCulloughs even more than they already do."

"I am nae lookin' for their love or adoration," Lachlan said drolly. "I only want their fealty."

Caelen nodded in agreement. "Then ye have a long and treacherous road ahead of ye."

Lachlan pushed himself to his feet. "Then I should get started as soon as possible."

"Then ye'll be wantin' to speak with their leader," Caelen informed him as he too, got to his feet. "Murdoch Chisolm."

TWO OF CAELEN'S MEN LED THE WAY OUT OF THE GATHERING ROOM and down a long and winding dark corridor. Lachlan, his men, along with Caelen, followed behind. As they walked down the corridor, their shadows danced in the torchlight along the stone walls.

Caelen's instincts were on high alert, one hand resting on the hilt of the dirk he kept in his belt. The hallway was far too narrow for sword battle, but one never knew when someone might attack.

As soon as the door was pulled open, odors from the dungeon swept through. Musty air, blended with the scent of urine and feces was enough to make Lachlan's eyes water.

One at a time they took the twisting stone staircase, into the bowels of the keep. The smell only grew worse as they descended the damp, moss covered stairs.

The dungeon was not at all as he had expected considering what he thought he knew about the Chisolms. There were no torture devices, no man in a black hood who would mete out punishments or try to extract information from enemies. Nay, 'twas a small space with only four small cells lined with heavy, black iron bars.

But those rooms were filled to capacity with men. Men who bore particularly furious expressions aimed directly at those they considered to be interlopers. Men of varying ages and sizes glowered at Lachlan's group.

Lachlan made his way to the front of the line. "Which one of ye is Murdoch Chisolm?"

One man, who Lachlan estimated to be in his late forties with a beard that went to his waist, stepped forward. He pressed his face between two iron bars. "I be Murdoch Chisolm," he declared. His hands and face were grimy, his dirty long hair fell way beyond his shoulders.

Lachlan didn't believe him for a moment. Neither did he believe the dozens of other men who stepped forward to declare themselves to be the man he was seeking.

"Pipe down, ye bloody bastards," one of Caelen's men shouted as he went to the last cell on the left. "Back away," he ordered the men lining the iron bars.

At first, the men refused. But the threat of castration made them part the seas so to speak.

There, in the far corner, was Murdoch Chisolm. Lachlan was certain 'twas he, for he was the only one not claiming the identity. Murdoch sat with his back against the wall with one leg stretched out across the dirty stone floor. He had one wrist resting on the bent knee, his free hand picking invisible lint from his filthy brown shirt.

"Him," Lachlan said to his men with a nod toward the one he assumed was Murdoch. He said nothing more as he turned and left the dungeon.

⁂

ONCE THEY WERE BACK IN THE GATHERING ROOM, LACHLAN'S MEN pushed Murdoch into one of the chairs by the hearth. Unfazed by their open hostility, he simply smiled up at them.

"I am Lachlan MacCullough, cousin to Black Richard MacCullough," Lachlan said as he stood by the hearth.

"And where is the *MacCullough*?" Murdoch spit on the floor defiantly.

Lachlan ignored both the question and the insult of spitting on the MacCullough name. "*I* am the MacCullough. I am actin' on Black Richard's behalf. I will be yer laird and chief."

'Twas quite apparent that Murdoch was unimpressed. "Just because ye say it is so does nae mean it is."

Lachlan had to admire the man's fealty to his own people, for he felt much the same way when the Chisolms took his own keep all those years ago. But the situations were vastly different.

"When Maitland Chisolm raided our keep nearly six years ago, he assumed 'twould be the end of the MacCulloughs." Lachlan leaned against the table and crossed his arms over his chest. "But he was wrong." He took a moment to study Murdoch closely. The man was close to his own age, with dark brown hair and pale blue eyes. Eyes that were, at this very moment, filled with malice and hatred. "When the former MacRay laird broke their generations-old alliance with the MacCulloughs, they too, thought 'twould be the end of us. And when Randall left Raibeart MacCullough for dead after kidnapping my cousins and friend, those too, were grave mistakes."

Murdoch yawned and stretched. "What be yer point in this walk down memory lane?"

"My point is that many a Chisolm before ye has underestimated the fierceness, the tenacity, and the will of the MacCullough clan." He let the words sink in for a long moment. "Bigger, wiser men than ye have nae lived to tell the tale. Consider this a warnin', Murdoch: dunnae underestimate me or mine. To do so is akin to signin' yer own death warrant."

LACHLAN LEFT NO DOUBT IN MURDOCH'S MIND THAT HE MEANT what he said. He gave the order for his men to round up every last Chisolm and bring them to the courtyard forthwith. There was no better time than now to inform these people who he was and what their choices were.

"What about those in the dungeon?" Fergus asked.

"Them as well."

With a nod, Fergus left to do his laird's bidding. But not before securely tying Murdoch to his chair.

"Ye will ne'er get them to accept ye," Murdoch called out from his seat near the dais.

Lachlan wanted to wipe the smirk off the man's face but maintained control of his temper. But just barely. "Then they will suffer the consequences."

Lachlan went about giving more orders. "Find out who the steward is and bring him to me," he told Jamie. "I also want the kitchen staff brought to me."

Jamie gave a nod of his head and left the gathering room to see to the tasks.

"Ye should leave now," Murdoch said. "While yer head is still attached to yer shoulders."

Lachlan ignored him as he took a seat at the dais. With his arms behind his head and his feet upon the table, he waited patiently for those he'd summoned to arrive. He made a mental list of all the things that needed to be done. First and foremost at the moment would be finding the steward and the Chisolm coffers.

THE COURTYARD WAS FILLED WITH CHISOLMS, ALL EAGER TO GET A glimpse of their captors. Nary a one of them considered the MacCulloughs as rightful laird, chief, or master. 'Twas clearly apparent by the scornful glares and hostility aimed at the MacCullough, McDunnah, and MacDougal men.

Even after Jamie came to tell him all were assembled, Lachlan remained in the gathering room. Murdoch had been silent for the past hour, pretending to have fallen asleep. Lachlan didn't believe it for a moment. No doubt the man was listening to every word whispered or openly spoken, trying to size up Lachlan and his men. He'd be doing the very same were their roles reversed.

After waiting what he considered to be a goodly amount of time, Lachlan ordered Murdoch released and taken to the courtyard with the others.

"Keep a close eye on him and his men," he whispered to Fergus.

Lachlan waited a few moments more before leaving the gathering room. The tall exterior doors were open and he could see the crowd.

These are my people, he thought. *They just dinnae realize it yet.*

He stepped to the edge of the wide landing and looked out at the gathering.

"I am Lachlan MacCullough, cousin to Black Richard MacCullough," he called out to the throng of people. "I act in Black Richard's stead. I am yer new laird and chief."

"Ye are nae *my* laird!" someone called out from the middle of the group. The group applauded and shouted their agreements.

"And where is Black Richard?" Someone else shouted. "Be he too much of a coward to show his face here?"

'Twas one of the MacDougall men who stepped forward to answer the man's insult. He pushed the man to the damp earth. "Would ye be brave enough to say that to his face?"

Stunned into muteness, the man lay on the ground staring up at him.

Insulted by what they perceived to be mistreatment, the crowd began clamoring and moving toward the MacDougall warrior. For every Chisolm who stepped forward, another of Lachlan's men responded. Soon a wall of warriors were in place, shouting threats to the horde.

"Enough!" Lachlan shouted from atop the steps.

He needed only call the order once. The crowd quieted and turned their attention back to Lachlan.

"I act in Richard's stead," Lachlan began. "Richard is meeting with the King."

He didn't believe he owed any of them an explanation as to where Richard was. However, if he mentioned Richard's impending meeting with David II, he felt it might add some validity to their claim against the Chisolms.

"What right do ye have to take our lands?" someone else shouted.

He felt his temper rising but would not fall prey to it. These people were trying to goad him into acting like a menacing fool. "By the laws of war," he called out his answer.

A low murmur began to grow. If he didn't get matters into hand now, he never would.

"Unlike yer former lairds, we dunnae kill innocents. We dunnae slaughter the defenseless," Lachlan shouted over the din. He was hoping to quell the murmurs. Instead, they only grew.

"Maitland would never do such a thing!" one person shouted. "And neither would Randall!" someone else shouted.

Taking in a deep breath, Lachlan shouted down the crowd. "Unlike the treatment yer former lairds gave our people, ye will be given a choice."

Hundreds of curious people stared back at him.

"Ye may stay or ye may go."

He gave his statement a moment to sink in. "If ye stay, ye will swear yer fealty to the MacCullough. Ye will be afforded the protection of the MacCullough clan and its allies."

"Bah! We already have allies!" a voice called out.

"If ye mean the Farquars," Lachlan said, searching for the man who protested, "their allegiance can only be purchased." He found the man in question, and looked at him directly. "They have already fled. If ye mean the MacGregors, we have an emissary meeting with their laird right now. If ye mean the MacRays, they have already sworn their allegiance to the MacCulloughs. That leaves ye with no one."

A low murmur washed over the large crowd. 'Twas apparent from some of the confused expressions staring back at him, that they were unaware of this bit of information.

"The MacCulloughs have the might of the McDunnahs, the MacDougalls, the MacRays, as well as the Mackintoshes and Grahams to stand behind them." He didn't bother explaining that their primary goal was a united Scotland.

"If ye wish to leave, ye may leave. Ye may take yer personal belongins with ye but ye will forever be banned from returning to these lands."

Lachlan gave one final, slow look at the people below. "Ye have one hour to make yer decision. If ye decide to leave, ye must be gone by the noonin' hour. If ye stay, ye will come to me to declare yer fealty."

And with that, he spun around and went back into the keep.

Chapter Four

It had been days since Keevah had slept and she was not alone in her exhaustion. 'Twasn't just her thoughts of Lachlan that kept her awake. Each night, the entire keep was awakened to the sounds of Colyne's plaintive wails - screams caused by nightmares. Nightmares he swore he could not recall.

But Keevah doubted the boy was being honest with anyone, least of all himself. No, she was quite certain he could remember every vivid detail of the dreams that haunted him. But for an 11-year-old child, it was difficult at times, to face the truth.

'Twas just as difficult for the adults in the keep to face it. Aeschene would sit with him, night after night, holding his hand, soothing him back to sleep.

Richard, although he was still healing from the beating he'd received during his time as a prisoner of Randall Chisolm, paced back and forth, night after night, waiting for the screams to begin. Richard remembered all too well the time in his life when nightmares haunted him. His heart ached for his youngest brother.

Raibeart paced right along with him.

What no one seemed to be doing was *talking* to the child during the daylight hours. To Keevah's way of thinking, that was, mayhap, not the best route to take. She believed that one needed to face a problem head on rather than sweep it away as if it didn't exist.

A week had passed with no improvement.

After breaking their fast on this bright, crisp November morn, she was able to convince Colyne to leave the keep under the guise of needing his help to retrieve her yarn. 'Twas not easy getting him to agree to help and not because he didn't wish to. The lad was simply too afraid to leave the safe confines of his home.

"I promise ye we will nae be long," she told him. 'Twas only after she told him he could carry her *sgian dubh* that he finally agreed.

They walked in silence through the courtyard. They paused just outside the gates whilst Colyne carefully studied the landscape around them.

"Black Richard has tripled the guard," she told him encouragingly. "And now that we own the Chisolm keep and all their holdings, I doubt we shall run into any trouble."

He gave the matter some thought before nodding his head and taking that first, all important step forward. Keevah gave him a warm smile and a reassuring pat on his shoulder.

As they took the path, with Colyne's eyes piercing their surroundings, Keevah felt certain her earlier assumptions had been correct.

They walked in silence the remainder of the way to her cottage. She opened the door and allowed Colyne to step inside first.

There was a week's worth of dust lining those possessions she had left behind; her bed, her little table and stool, as well as her kitchen accouterments.

Days ago, Richard had sent three of his men with her to retrieve her loom. It now sat near the hearth in the gathering room. She had also gathered most of her yarn and she had been too busy since to come back for the rest.

"Colyne, would ye mind if we sat and talked for a moment?" she asked as she sat on the stool next to the cold brazier.

Worry flashed in his eyes. She could see that he wanted nothing more than to hurry back to the keep. "I promise, we will nae tarry long. I simply want to talk to ye."

He raised a dubious brow. "Talk to me?"

"Aye," she smiled warmly. "I want to talk about the bad dreams ye have been having."

He shrugged his shoulders and diverted his gaze, a habit that was becoming increasingly irksome. "I cannae remember them. Please, can we go back now?"

"Colyne, 'tis all right for ye to be afraid. I reckon I'd be havin' bad dreams of my own had I gone through what ye did."

He remained silent and continued to stare at his feet.

"Mayhap if ye were to talk about it, ye might feel better."

"What is there to talk about?" he murmured. "Because of me, me brothers almost died."

"Because of ye?" she shook her head. "Nay, Colyne, ye did nothin' wrong."

Anger began to bubble up to the surface. "Had I stayed closer to the keep instead of lookin' for that stupid treasure, no one would have gotten hurt!"

"Oh, Colyne, lad, that is nae true. People were hurt because of what Randall Chisolm did. People were hurt because of that man's black heart."

He glowered at her angrily. "They were hurt because of me!"

Keevah rushed across the floor and pulled him into her bosom. "Nay, Colyne. I swear to ye that is nae true. If ye dunnae believe me, ye should ask Richard."

Tears began to fall down his cheeks. "He hates me. So does Raibeart," he cried against her chest.

Her heart cracked at his anguish. "No one hates ye, lad."

"Aye, they do!" he cried. "They are just too polite to say it."

She could not resist the urge to laugh. "Polite? Black Richard? Raibeart?" she shook her head. "I have never heard anyone accuse either of them of bein' polite."

He didn't find her statement amusing and told her so.

Crouching down, she took him by his shoulders and looked directly into his eyes. "Listen to me, Colyne. Ye did nothin' wrong. No one hates ye. We all love and adore ye."

He wiped his tears away with the palms of his hands. "But-"

"But *nothin'*," she interrupted, refusing to listen to his argument.

"Ye did nothin' wrong, lad. Not a thing. Have I ever lied to ye?"

Scrunching his brow, he thought on it for a long moment. "Nay," he admitted solemnly.

"Now, I will not have ye worryin' over this any longer. Ye, lad, are loved beyond measure. This, I promise to ye. When ye are older, ye will be better able to understand all that has happened to ye. But for now, will ye please try to set yer worry aside?"

He smiled, not quite as bright and innocent as before, but at least he smiled. "Aye, Keevah, I promise."

OCTOBER HAD COME AND GONE WITH QUIET EASE. THE REMNANTS of autumn with its vibrant shades of crimson, goldenrod, and burgundy now peeked through the dust of the first snow.

It had been more than a month since Keevah had last seen Lachlan, his promise to return home in a sennight not kept. Deep down, she knew she shouldn't have expected him to be able to keep that promise, for he was far too busy still trying to bring the Chisolms to heel.

He had sent missives to Richard, updating him on the progress he was making, which, according to the bits and pieces Aeschene shared with her, was not much. 'Twas important business he was tending to and it sounded as though he was exceedingly busy and occupied.

Keevah hadn't changed her mind about declining his marriage proposal. Nay, that was still out of the question. Still, she had hoped that once, just once, he might have inserted a small message, just for her. While she couldn't have read that message to save her life, she would have relished knowing he was at least thinking of her. She certainly couldn't get him out of her mind no matter how hard she tried.

Her days were spent being Aeschene's eyes; helping her get from one place to another within the keep. Truly, she enjoyed the woman's company, nay, her friendship and was glad for it.

Richard's and Raibeart's injuries from their ordeal with Randall Chisolm's men had long ago healed. Colyne was making progress as well. Speaking to his brothers and gaining their reassurance that he was not to blame for what had happened with the Randall had done wonders for the boy's spirit.

Still, he held on to the fear of stepping beyond the walls of their keep. No longer did he play with the other children. Instead, he kept inside. Each afternoon he spent with Marisse who now acted as his tutor. She marveled on more than one occasion on his progress. "He reads better than I," she told Richard and Aeschene one chilly winter day. "And he is wicked with his cypherin'. I've never seen the like before."

No one was more proud than Richard. While he was still greatly concerned over Colyne's refusal to play with the other children or to go more than a few feet beyond the doors of the keep, he was mightily proud of the lad's intelligence.

Richard waited until Marisse had left for the day before pulling Colyne into his private study.

"Am I in trouble?" Colyne asked sheepishly.

"Nay," Richard replied with a fond smile.

"Ye usually only bring me here when I have done somethin' wrong," Colyne politely reminded him.

"I believe yer mischief-filled days are long gone, are they nae?"

Colyne nodded as he glanced about the room nervously.

"I brought ye here to tell ye how verra proud I am of ye," Richard began as he leaned back in his chair. "Of all the MacCullough men, out of all my brothers, ye seem to be the only one who could master his studies."

Colyne looked at him as if to say he thought he was mad, or over exaggerating.

"'Tis true," Richard said. "Marisse claims ye to be intelligent beyond yer years."

"It really is nae that hard," he said with a roll of his eyes.

"Mayhap for ye it is easy, but not everyone can claim such," he said.

They sat in silence for a short time, with Colyne fidgeting in his seat.

"Colyne, I think it is time ye start yer trainin'."

His head shot up so fast Richard was surprised it didn't give him an ache. His mouth fell open and his eyes widened.

"On the morrow, ye shall train with Raibeart and I, in the courtyard."

"But I thought I had to wait until I was older?" he exclaimed.

Richard chuckled. "I said that at a time when ye were still behavin' like a hellion. Ye have changed these past few months, and for the better."

Colyne's face fell as it burned crimson. Lowering his head, he said, "I lost my sword."

"Yer wooden one?" Richard asked.

He gave a curt nod. "When the Chisolms took us. I broke it when I hit the Chisolm in his head."

Richard threw his head back and laughed heartily. "Och, lad, ye will make a verra fine warrior."

Scrunching his brow, Colyne asked what he meant by that.

"Ye defended yerself, Colyne. Ye fought a man twice as old and twice as strong as ye. And ye broke yer wooden sword over his skull. I could nae be more proud."

Richard could have given an entire slew of reasons why he was choosing to start Colyne's training early. But the most important one was to give the young boy the confidence he needed to face his demons. And if there was one thing Richard knew all too well, it was fighting demons. 'Twas bad enough to do as a man full-grown. He could only imagine the torment his younger brother was suffering.

"We begin on the morrow," Richard informed him. "Do ye think ye are ready?"

Colyne thought long and hard before giving a nod of his head. "Aye, Richard, I think I am."

Truth be told, Colyne wasn't sure he was ready to begin his training. But if the man he admired most in this world felt he was, then, he supposed, that had to mean something.

He spent the remainder of the afternoon in his room, staring out the window. Raibeart had recovered nicely from his injuries and was off doing whatever it was his brother was fond of doing lately.

Colyne missed the old Raibeart. The brother who, until a few months ago, was his closest friend and confidant. For as long as he could remember, he and Raibeart never spent a moment apart. After the deaths of his father and other brothers, all they had were each other. Richard was too busy fending off starvation for their clan to spend any amount of time with them. Truly, Colyne didn't blame Richard for any of it. He understood that as chief, Richard's first duty was to his people.

So he and Raibeart were often left to their own devices, to raise themselves.

In trouble far more often than not, it didn't matter as long as the two of them were together.

But everything had changed when Richard married Aeschene.

Aye, most of it was for the better. No longer did they feel like outcasts in their own clan. Nay, each of them finally felt like they had a purpose and that they belonged.

Whilst those changes were for the better, there were other changes that Colyne didn't like. Such as bathing more than once a month. But more importantly, the changes taking place in his brother.

Raibeart no longer had the time for him. He was too busy training and *bein' a man,* as he often like to claim.

Colyne missed him.

He was mightily surprised, therefore, to find his brother waiting for him in the courtyard the following morning. There was something about the way the early morning light was shining down that made Colyne realize just how Raibeart was looking more and more like Richard. "Were ye plannin' on sleepin' the day away?" Raibeart asked, sounding most serious.

Colyne stopped and began to stammer out an apology. 'Twas then that Raibeart grinned most mischievously. "Dinnae fash yerself, brother. I was only jestin'."

Much relieved, Colyne's shoulders relaxed.

"Richard is delayed this morn," Raibeart said as they started toward the training fields. "But dinnae worry it, ye will be trainin' with me this morn."

For the first time in a very long while, Colyne actually smiled. How long had it been since the two of them actually spent any good amount of time together? Not wishing to waste a moment thinking on it, he raced to catch up to the brother he admired most in this world. 'Twas going to be a verra good day.

Chapter Five

Lachlan's skull ached incessantly. A malady he'd never suffered from until arriving at the Chisolm keep.

They'd been here for over a sennight and were no closer to gaining the fealty of the Chisolms than the day they'd first crossed through the massive walls of the keep.

'Twas just after the morning meal as he sat in his private study. A small room directly behind the gathering room, it had once been used for storing spare candles, dishes, linens and the like. He had refused to take over the former laird's large and opulently furnished study.

Thankfully, the roaring fire from the grand hearth on the opposite side of the wall gave off enough heat to warm the small space. There was barely enough room for the table he used as a desk, let alone a brazier. 'Twas even more cramped this morn as Jamie and Fergus sat in chairs across from him.

"Ye really must consider taking a larger room," Jamie said. "I cannae even stretch out my legs."

Lachlan resisted the urge to roll his eyes. "We are nae here for comfort," he admonished. "We are here to insure a successful transition for the future of Black Richard and Aeschene's bairn."

Jamie scoffed, for he'd heard those words far too many times in the past weeks. "I ken why we are here," he said. "But that does nae mean we have to live like monks."

To Lachlan's way of thinking, he needed to get rid of every reminder from any former lairds. He needed to show the Chisolm people that 'twas *he*, a MacCullough, who was in charge now.

Ignoring Jamie's complaint, he asked for their morning reports. He'd intentionally put Jamie in charge of gleaning information from the Chisolm womenfolk for various reasons. The primary one being Jamie had a reputation for wooing lasses. Although Lachlan couldn't see the appeal himself, most women found it difficult to turn away from Jamie's dark blue eyes and dimpled cheeks.

"I tell ye, Lachlan, I have ne'er met a more stubborn lot of women," Jamie said. "They are still loyal to Randall Chisolm and the man's been dead for weeks."

Fergus grunted. "Ye mean yer good looks and charm are nae workin' on the lasses?"

"I would nae say *that*," Jamie said with a grin. "As long as I can get them away from their mums for a few moments, I have nae problem finding what I need."

Fergus let out a weary sigh. "Yer physical needs are nae nearly as important as information."

Jamie chuckled. "And who says I cannae achieve both?"

Frustrated, Lachlan held up a hand. "I dunnae care *how* ye get the information. Just tell us what ye ken."

He sat up taller in his seat, scratched his stubbled jaw and began to divulge what he knew. "They still despise us bein' here," Jamie said.

That came as no surprise to any of them.

"Say what we will about Maitland and Randall bein' sons of whores and ruthless bastards. But ne'er once have their people gone without."

'Twas the same story they'd heard since arriving. There was not one Chisolm who would say a bad word against their former lairds.

"So how do we go about gaining their fealty?" Fergus asked.

That was the same question they'd been asking for weeks. Thus far, nothing was working.

"At least they've quit tryin' to poison us," Jamie offered.

"For now, they have," Lachlan said. "But could be naught more than a ploy to try to gain our trust."

Fergus agreed. "I trust none of them."

"If we could get rid of Murdoch ..." Jamie was once again subtly hinting at his firm belief they needed to hang Murdoch Chisolm.

While he was truly tempted at times to do just that, Lachlan still refused. "And make a martyr out of him?" he asked rhetorically with a shake of his head. "Nay."

"Ye either kill him or let him out of the dungeons," Fergus said. "The longer ye keep him there, the more these people will resist."

Lachlan gave the matter considerable consideration. His original intent had been to keep the men locked up until their spirits were broken and they'd finally acquiesce. Instead of breaking them, prison seemed to make them stronger. "Ye may be right," he said before chuckling. "They are nearly as stubborn as we are, aye?"

His statement garnered no argument from Fergus. Jamie, however, was reluctant to agree.

"Verra well," Lachlan said. "We shall let them out. Let them return to their wives and families. Maybe 'twill be looked upon as a gesture of good will."

"I give it a day before Murdoch begins another insurrection," Jamie said.

Lachlan smiled rather deviously. "Then 'twill give us a good reason to kill him, aye?"

That notion lifted all their spirits.

"Now, have we gotten a complete tally of the number of Chisolms?" Lachlan asked, moving on to other matters.

Fergus pulled a small bit of parchment from the pouch on his belt. He carefully unfolded it and read his accounting. "Including the prisoners below, there are two-hundred and seven warriors of varying ages and degrees of skill. One-hundred and seventy-two of them are married. We have one-hundred and eighty-seven bairns and weans, and countless women who are with child. There are also thirty-seven lasses who are of marryin' age and forty-nine lads ready to train."

"Good, lord!" Lachlan exclaimed. He hadn't realized just how large the Chisolm clan was.

Fergus gave a curt nod but looked at odds with something.

"What about the elderly and infirm?" Lachlan asked.

"I was just about to get to that," Fergus said. "There are none."

Puzzled, Lachlan asked for clarification.

"'Tis as I am tellin' ye, Lachlan. I can find no one over the age of fifty. No one who is ill, on the verge of death, no one I would consider elderly. I cannae even find a man missin' a finger. 'Tis the oddest thing I have e'er seen."

"I have noticed that as well," Jamie said. "I have nae seen anyone with even the slightest limp."

The hairs on the back of Lachlan's neck stood on end. "And have ye made inquiries into this oddity?"

Fergus rolled his eyes. "Of course, I have," he replied. "And ye can well imagine the response. No one will speak of it."

Something dark niggled at the back of his mind. There could be no good and sound reason for such an anomaly.

"Did ye count the two women who live in the woods?" Jamie asked Fergus.

Fergus furrowed his brow. "I have," he replied.

"What two women?" Lachlan asked.

"Accordin' to some, there are two young women who live in the woods. They be nae of their right minds. The clan shunned them long ago," Fergus explained.

"Shunned them?" Lachlan asked with a raised brow. "For what reason?"

Fergus shifted uncomfortably in his chair. "For nae bein' of sound mind."

"There must be more to it than that," Lachlan said, clearly appalled by the notion.

"Some say they be witches," Jamie added.

"Are they a danger to themselves or others?" Lachlan asked.

Jamie shook his head. "I honestly dunnae ken, Lachlan. All anyone will tell us is that they were shunned years ago because they were 'odd' and nae of sound mind."

"Odd? Nae of sound mind?" Lachlan was incredulous.

"They are also convinced those verra woods are haunted. From what I have learned, nae a soul has so much has set a toe inside it in decades."

"Haunted?" The ache in his head increased.

Jamie scratched his stubble jaw. "That is what they believe. Filled with witches and fairies and ghosts."

"Fetch me the steward," he said, directing the order to Fergus simply because he was closest to the door.

WALTER CHISOLM WAS A MAN OF FEW WORDS.

He now sat opposite his new laird in Lachlan's very cramped study. Any fool could see the man was as nervous as a whore in church. His Adam's apple bobbed up and down repeatedly as he did his best to hide his trembling hands.

Walter was a tall, slender man with thinning light brown hair. He'd tried to hide the fact that he was losing the aforementioned hair by combing one side over at an extreme angle before sweeping it forward to cover his forehead. Lachlan wondered if any of the Chisolms had the heart to tell the poor man he looked utterly ridiculous.

"Have ye found the missing books yet?" Lachlan asked. He hadn't thought he sounded too harsh, but Walter very nearly jumped out of his own skin. 'Twas a question he'd been asking since the first day of his arrival. Thus far, Walter was unable to 'locate' them. Swearing they must have been lost or destroyed during the invasion of the interlopers - better known as the McDunnahs and MacCulloughs.

"N-Nay," he replied before swallowing hard for the umpteenth time.

Lachlan didn't believe him. He hadn't believed him the first dozen or so times he claimed not to know the whereabouts of the Chisolm accountings, journals, and other documents in question. That was why he'd put Fergus and a few other men on the task of finding them.

"Ye're quite certain?" Lachlan asked.

"Quite certain."

He knew the man was lying, but Walter was unaware of the fact. For nearly a fortnight, they'd been trying to get an accounting of the

Chisolm's assets and debts. Walter, the steward for the former laird, should have been the one person who knew what was what and who was who. Thus far, he'd fought every attempt Lachlan had made at asking nicely.

Lachlan stood up from his desk and walked to the door. "Would ye be surprised, Walter, to learn that I have found the books and ledgers?" he asked as he opened the door. Jamie and Fergus walked in, each with a crate filled with journals and ledgers. Carefully, they set the items on the table in front of Walter.

"'Twas absolutely amazin' where we found them," Lachlan said as he watched from near the door. "These we found hidden in a secret space behind the wall of yer room."

Two more men entered the room, each with a crate filled with more of the accountings. "These we found hidden in the stables."

As soon as they left, two more men entered. Between them, a heavy trunk. "And aye, we found the coffers. Hidden in the granary."

After the last men left, Lachlan closed the door. "Now, why do ye reckon all of these verra important documents and yer gold were scattered hither and yon?"

Walter rather resembled a fish trying to catch a worm. His mouth opened and shut several times as he fought to come up with a plausible explanation.

Lachlan had reached the end of his patience. He slammed a heavy fist down on top of the only empty space left on his desk. "Damn it, man!" he barked. "I have had enough of ye and the rest of yer people behavin' like spoiled brats!"

Walter had jumped at the fist hitting the desk. He jumped in his seat again when Lachlan began to shout.

"I am nae yer enemy. I am yer laird and chief. And it is high time ye and every one of ye begin to see it, lest I cast the lot of ye out!"

The man couldn't find the wherewithal or the courage to reply.

Lachlan took in a steadying breath. "Walter, I wish ye no ill will, I truly dunnae. I would rather work with ye, to bring order to this clan. I will give ye two days to think about whether or not ye'd like to work with me or if ye'd like to be banished from the clan."

Stunned, his mouth fell agape as his eyes grew wide and round. "Banished?"

"Aye. Banished."

Lachlan stood to his full height. "The choice is yers, Walter. I suggest ye think long and hard. Ye are dismissed."

Walter got to his feet and hurried from the room.

After the door closed, Lachlan turned his attention to Jamie. "I want ye to bring Murdoch to me."

"To discuss his decision to stay?"

Lachlan shook his head. "Nay. To discuss his surrender."

IT HAD TAKEN FERGUS AND JAMIE NEARLY THREE HOURS TO FIND Murdoch Chisolm. Once word had spread that his presence was required before their new laird, the clan began a grand game of hide and find.

They found him all right. Hiding in a secret space in the attic of the granary. Fergus believed it a most egregious and cowardly thing to do. Jamie was of the belief 'twas just another game the Chisolms liked to play; aggravate the bloody hell out of the MacCulloughs until they left out of sheer frustration.

After dragging him from the dark hiding space, Fergus forced the man to the ladder.

"Hidin' like a coward," Fergus said through gritted teeth as he watched the man slink down the ladder. "After all yer braggin' about yer bravery." He was truly and thoroughly disgusted.

"I was nae hidin'," Murdoch argued. "'Tis me favorite place to nap. Nice and quiet."

Jamie waited until Fergus climbed down before taking Murdoch by one arm. Fergus took the other.

"I say cowardice," Fergus said as they walked toward the keep.

"I would have to agree," Jamie said.

Murdoch laughed at the accusation. "I wager ye a hundred sillars I could best both of ye with one arm tied behind my back."

Jamie and Fergus glanced at one another before breaking into riotous laughter. "Says the man who has been hidin' like a frightened bird for three hours."

"I've seen braver newborn lambs," Fergus added as they thundered angrily across the yard. Chickens squawked and scattered and people glowered as they made their way toward the keep.

"Ye will see," Murdoch told them. "Soon enough, ye shall see."

Chapter Six

Lachlan was waiting for them in the gathering room. Sitting in a chair at the long table on the dais, he took a sip of ale - MacCullough ale- as they were still untrusting of the Chisolms. He watched the men come into the room.

Fergus and Jamie brought Murdoch forward, neither letting loose their grip on the man's arms.

"Found him hidin' in the granary," Fergus told him. "Like the coward he is."

Murdoch shook his head with a good measure of disinterest. "I told ye, I was merely nappin'."

Lachlan glared across the table. "I have had enough of yer games," Lachlan told him. "A fortnight ago, ye said ye wished to stay. But ye have yet to swear yer fealty," the laird reminded him. "Why did ye nae leave with the others?"

More than fifty warriors, along with wives and children, had left the day he had given them the choice. But Murdoch had chosen to stay. Lachlan was by no means a stupid man. He knew from the first moment he met the man he'd have to watch him carefully.

"This is my home," Murdoch told him pointedly.

"Then ye will give me yer fealty?" Lachlan was certain he already knew the answer. Even if Murdoch agreed, there was a strong possibility 'twould be naught more than empty words.

"If ye want my fealty, MacCullough, ye will need to earn it."

His statement surprised Lachlan. He had anticipated a worthless promise. "I challenge ye, MacCullough. I challenge ye."

T HE CHALLENGE WASN'T SURPRISING IN AND OF ITSELF. WHAT Lachlan did find astonishing was the strength behind the words, the tone of his voice, and the way he stood, tall and proud—with conviction.

"Ye think ye could best me in battle?" Lachlan asked with a raised brow.

Pulling his shoulders back, Murdoch nodded his head slowly. "Aye, I do. Ye are nae wanted here, MacCullough. None of ye are."

"We earned the right to be here, Murdoch. We did nae start the war betwixt our clans; Maitland Chisolm did. Ye have no one to blame for this but he."

Murdoch scoffed openly. "Maitland did what was best for his people. He had every right to retaliate."

Puzzled, Lachlan took a step forward. "Retaliate? Against the MacCulloughs?" He was utterly confused. "Pray, tell me, what exactly did the MacCulloughs do that necessitated retaliation?"

The look Murdoch gave Lachlan said he thought him no smarter than a flea. With a groan of disgust, he said, "When yer men attacked us like cowards."

Lachlan's brow furrowed in confusion.

"Near on seven years ago, Galen MacCullough sent a band of his warriors to our southern border. In the middle of the night, thirty of yer men killed five of our young men who patrolled the border." Anger burned behind his eyes. His voice grew deeper, filled with repugnance. "After that, they made their way onto our lands and killed an innocent family of six. Set their home ablaze. Raped the young mother of four as they made her husband and children watch. *That* is why we retaliated."

Repulsed at the notion, Lachlan ground his teeth together before responding. "I tell ye we never did such a thing. Never."

"Tell that to the dead," Murdoch seethed.

Shaking his head, Lachlan took another step closer. "Galen MacCullough was a good and honorable man. He would never order such a thing. What proof do ye have?"

Crossing his arms over his chest, "There," he said with a nod toward the hearth behind Lachlan. "On the mantle is a box. Inside that box is a letter from Galen MacCullough. Written in his own hand."

Fergus retrieved the box from the mantle and placed it on the table next to Lachlan.

"Maitland kept that letter as a reminder to all of us why we should hate and despise every one of ye. There is yer proof."

Lachlan lifted the lid with his index finger. Inside the box was a rolled parchment. Carefully, he removed it, unrolled it, and began to read quietly.

Maitland,

I write this to ye in my own hand so there is no mistake as to the meaning or contents.

Consider this attack a warning to ye and yers. Ye have betrayed the MacCulloughs in the worst possible way. I will never forgive ye for what ye have done.

Therefore, I officially declare war upon ye and yers.

I will nae rest until every last Chisolm is obliterated from this earth. I will see to it yer name and every memory of ye is erased from history.

Ye have been warned.

Galen MacCullough

Lachlan read the missive twice. He knew his uncle's handwriting well enough to know it was not written in his own hand.

"Galen MacCullough did nae write this."

Murdoch's expression said enough; he didn't believe him. "Ye lie."

Fergus and Jamie stepped forward, swords drawn, ready to gut the man for the insult.

"Stand down," Lachlan ordered in a low, even tone.

Both men continued to glower at Murdoch and only took one step away.

"Galen MacCullough was my uncle," Lachlan began. "I could pick his hand out from a hundred others. This is nae his."

"But it says—"

"I ken what it says," Lachlan interrupted. "But I swear to ye, 'twas nae written by Galen MacCullough. It does nae even sound like him."

Murdoch eyed him suspiciously for a long while. "Do ye sincerely expect me to believe ye?"

"I dunnae care what ye believe, Murdoch. I speak the truth. Galen did nae write this."

"Then who did?"

FOR THE LIFE OF HIM, LACHLAN DIDN'T KNOW. BUT HE HAD A sneaking suspicion. "Mayhap someone who wanted us at war with one another."

Reluctantly, Murdoch gave it a measure of thought. "I ken no one who would do such a thing. No one."

"Think of who benefited most from a war betwixt our clans," Lachlan said. He leaned back against the edge of the table and crossed his arms over his chest and allowed the man time to consider what he'd said.

After a long while, Murdoch shook his head again and raised his empty palms in defeat. "Ye will have to explain it to me, MacCullough. I can think of no one."

"How long did it take for the MacRay to come to ye after the attack?"

Murdoch scratched his jaw as he thought on it. "I dunnae ken. 'Twas nae long I reckon. Walter would ken better than I."

"Yer steward, Walter Chisolm?"

"Aye, him."

The two men sized each other up for a spell before Murdoch finally broke the silence. "Do ye honestly wish me to believe the MacRay is behind this?"

Lachlan shrugged his shoulders again. "As I said before, I dunnae care what ye believe. I for one would like to ken the truth of it."

"Mayhap 'twas another MacCullough."

The thought *had* entered his mind, but he immediately dismissed it. "I ken of nae MacCulloughs who would stoop to such treachery. Nay," he said shaking his head in disbelief. "Nay, 'twas nae MacCullough. But I am determined to get to the bottom of it."

There was still a good amount of skepticism to be found in Murdoch's eyes.

"Do ye still wish to challenge me?" Lachlan asked.

"Damned right I do."

A DARE IS A DARE IS A DARE. AT LEAST IN THE MIND OF ANY GOOD Scots lad. One couldn't back down on a dare, or so nine-year-old Gylbeart Chisolm believed. He was just as strong as his da and older brothers; his mother had told him so only that very morning.

So when ten-year-old Inan Chisolm accused Gylbeart of being too afraid to go climb the tallest and oldest oak tree, well, 'twas a challenge he could not let go unfulfilled.

The group of three lads and one lass made their way across the open field behind their homes and into a very small forest. Just near the edge, sat the infamous tree. "It must be as old as God," little Maldouen Chisolm said in awe. He tried to whistle, but he was only seven and his two front teeth were missing.

Mariam Chisolm was the oldest of the group at eleven years. A bright, sweet lass with golden blonde locks and bright blue eyes. "Ye will fall and break yer neck," she warned the lads. "Yer mum would skelp yer hide if she kent ye're even thinkin' of doin' this."

The boys, as most young boys do, ignored her warnings.

Gylbeart brushed his curly brown hair from his forehead, spat into the palms of his hands and rubbed them together. A moment later, he began his attempt to climb the auld tree. But try as he might, he couldn't quite reach the first low hanging limb.

"See?" Mariam said as she placed her hands on her hips. "Ye be too short."

Undeterred, Maldouen came up with the next brilliant idea. "Here," he said as he got down on all fours directly under the large limb. "Stand on my back and reach."

"This is a bad idea," Mariam warned.

"If ye dunnae want to watch, then go home," Maldouen told her.

Gylbeart crawled onto Maldouen's back and carefully stood up. "Dunnae move so much," he scolded his friend.

"'Tis nay me, ye daft badger. Ye be the one wigglin' like a worm."

Uncertainty filled young Inan's eyes as he came to stand nearer to Mariam. "He is verra brave," he muttered under his breath as Gylbeart grabbed the low tree limb. 'Twas far too fat to wrap his hands around it entirely. "Stand up, Maldouen," he said. "Boost me up a bit farther."

With a good deal of caution, Maldouen moved backward a bit so that his shoulders were directly under Gylbeart's feet. With a grunt and a groan, he stood upright, pushing his friend higher and higher in the process.

With a sigh of relief, Gylbeart was able to pull himself up and onto the fat, rough limb.

"I kenned he could do it," Inan declared with a smile.

"See?" Gylbeart said, puffing with pride. "I told ye I am nay scared."

"Bah!" Maldouen said. "That is nae verra far."

Taking the comment as another challenge, Gylbeart studied the tree closely before grabbing the nearest limb. Not quite as fat as the one he stood on, he was able to grab hold and pull himself up.

Before anyone realized it, the boy was a good ten to twelve feet off the ground.

Mariam shook her head. Inan cheered and threw his fist into the air. Maldouen pretended not to be impressed. "Och! Anyone could climb that high," he said with a dismissive wave of his hand.

Excited that he'd come this far, Gylbeart decided to climb higher. Higher and higher until the branches had grown far too small to offer any support. In his nine-year-old mind, he was at least three hundred feet off the ground. In truth, 'twas closer to fifty. Still, 'twas awfully high for such a young and small lad.

"Come down now," Mariam called up to him. Turning to scowl at Maldouen, she yelled, "Ye have proven ye can do it."

Even Maldouen had to admit he was impressed.

Gylbeart gave a loud hoot of victory before he began his descent back to the safety of the ground. Admittedly, 'twas easier climbing up than down, but he was feeling far too proud of himself to confess to any worries.

He'd just reached the fat limb where his journey began. His foot slipped, his legs went out, and he landed on the limb hard on his bum. A frantic heartbeat later, he was falling backwards off the limb. He turned midair and tried to brace himself for the fall.

Mariam screamed.

Maldouen gasped.

Inan almost wet himself.

He heard the crack of a bone breaking in his right hand right before his world went black.

TWO WARRIORS STOOD FACING ONE ANOTHER ON THE SNOW-covered ground. Each man just as determined as the other to claim victory.

Snow crunched under their deerskin boots. Sunlight glistened off bare skin, swords, and maces.

They were surrounded by at least one hundred onlookers - most, of course, hoping for Murdoch to come out victorious. The Chisolms were clearly of the belief the battle wouldn't last long and soon, they'd be able to rid their keep and lands of the MacCulloughs. Their smiles and whispers said as much.

'Twas Murdoch who moved first, swinging his sword in a wide arc. Lachlan knew 'twas naught more than a test, to see how he'd respond. Lachlan didn't move. He kept his feet firmly planted on the ground.

Murdoch was surprised by Lachlan's inaction; he had expected some sort of retaliation or response. He took a few steps sideways and swung again. And again, Lachlan didn't move.

Frustrated, he took two steps forward. This time, he decided to lunge forward, aiming for Lachlan's gut.

Anticipating this move, Lachlan stepped out of the way before the tip of his opponent's sword could land on its mark. As Murdoch moved forward, Lachlan stepped sideways and landed a hard blow to the back of the man's skull, sending him to the ground.

A loud gasp came up from the crowd.

Murdoch landed face first in the snow, rolled over quickly, and scurried to his feet. Furious, he swiped the wet snow from his face with the back of his hand and glowered.

Lachlan's expression didn't change. He continued to study the man closely. He could see his pulse throbbing in his neck, the sweat just beginning to form on his brow.

Murdoch might be the leader of the Chisolm resistance, but he was not the well-trained warrior Lachlan had been led to believe. However, an untrained warrior could be even more dangerous than one who had been well trained. Either by accident or sheer luck.

A moment passed, then two. Murdoch lunged forward again with the same move. Lachlan responded just as he had moments ago.

After Murdoch's third failed attempt at lunging, Lachlan rolled his eyes. He stood over Murdoch who was lying on his back in the cold snow. "Mayhap ye would like to train a few months with my men?"

Fuming, Murdoch rolled to his feet. "I would rather die."

"As ye wish," Lachlan said right before he swiped the tip of his blade across Murdoch's chest. 'Twasn't a deep cut or grievous wound, but it did bleed.

Stunned, Murdoch was frozen in place and was unable to respond to the next swing of Lachlan's sword. It sliced through the tender flesh of Murdoch's arm. Blood began to trickle down instantly. The pain caused him to let loose his grip on his sword. It fell to the ground, crunching into the snow.

Before Lachlan could ask the man if he was done with this foolish attempt to challenge him, a most horrific sounding scream broke through the air. 'Twas an agonizing, guttural lamentation. The sound only a mother could make when she'd just lost a child.

Chapter Seven

Every man, woman, and child rushed toward the sound of anguish. Through the courtyard, out of the gates, and across a well-worn path they ran.

A crowd had gathered near the cottages. Lachlan, Jamie, and Fergus made their way through the throng of people. On the ground near one of the tidy little cottages, a woman held her young son: nine-year-old Gylbeart.

Lachlan breathed a heavy sigh of relief. From the wailing, he'd been certain someone had died. But the little boy was quite alive, if not a bit terrified and covered with scrapes and scratches.

"What be the matter?" Lachlan asked as he knelt next to the woman and child.

The woman couldn't stop crying long enough to explain. The more she cried, the more upset the boy became. "Please, dunnae cry, mum. Please, dunnae cry."

'Twas Mariam who stepped forward to explain what had transpired. "He fell from an oak tree."

Lachlan let out a chuckle while Fergus and Jamie smiled and shook their heads. "Och! That be nae reason to carry on so."

Mariam looked at him as though he were as intelligent as a rock. "But he broke his arm."

The seriousness of her tone made him smile a bit broader. "Well, I am certain the healer can fix it. He will be as right as rain in no time." He patted her head before turning his attention to the weeping mother.

"What be yer name?"

Too bereft and consumed with grief, she couldn't speak.

"Joan," Mariam informed him. "And that be Gylbeart."

Lachlan thanked the lass before turning back to the mother and son. "'Tis pleased I am to meet ye," he said with a warm smile. "Now, let me help ye get her son into yer cottage."

He scooped the little boy into his arms and stood. Gylbeart's eyes grew as wide as trenchers, awash in uncertainty.

"Now, which cottage is yers?" he asked the boy.

Stunned into muteness, 'twas Mariam who came to the rescue once again. "That one," she said as she pointed to one of the small cottages. "I will show ye."

Soon, she was opening the door and leading Lachlan inside.

'Twas a neat and tidy space and very much resembled most cottages. In the corner, ahead and on the left, was a nice sized bed Lachlan assumed belonged to the lad's parents. Carefully, he made his way past a large table, and the brazier, and gently laid the lad down.

When he turned around, Jamie and Fergus were standing on either side of the doorway. Two older women were helping to bring Joan inside. 'Twas all the poor woman could do not to fall to her knees. They sat her down at the table while one woman rushed to grab her a mug of cider. They sat on either side of her, patting her hands and offering what comfort they could.

Lachlan rolled his eyes in dismay. "Joan, yer son will be hale and hearty verra soon."

She glowered at him. She actually glowered at him. *Lord above, when will these people realize I am nae their enemy.*

"He has a *broken arm and hand*," she seethed.

"But 'tis nae a broken neck," Lachlan replied firmly. "Ye should be glad of *that*."

"'Twould have been better for all of us!" she cried angrily.

As appalled as he was confused, Lachlan stepped toward her. "How can ye say such a thing? He is just a little boy. How could ye wish death upon a poor child?"

Mariam made her way into the cottage and stood next to Lachlan. "Because death would be better than goin' away, ye ken?"

He most assuredly did not ken. Baffled, he stared down at the little girl. "Nay, lass, I dunnae ken what ye mean."

"Gylbeart will have to go away now," she said as if it made all the sense in the world.

It suddenly dawned on him then, what she meant. Horrified by the realization as to why there were no infirm, or elderly, or anyone with so much as a limp here.

"Ye cannae be serious," he muttered aghast.

"She is!" Joan shouted. "I will have to send me sweet boy away. Had he died, I could have a nice funeral. But I cannae do that now."

His stomach churned as disgust blended with anger. "Let me get this straight," he began with clenched teeth. "Anyone - including a little boy - who is infirm or aged or otherwise incapacitated, is sent away?"

Mariam and the women nodded, looking relieved that he finally understood.

Jamie and Fergus came to stand beside him. Onlookers stood just outside the cottage, trying to get a glimpse of what was taking place within.

"Are ye all mad?" Lachlan shouted.

M̲URMURS BROKE OUT AMONG THOSE STANDING OUTSIDE J̲OAN AND Andrew Chisolm's cottage.

Inside, three women and a little girl looked at Lachlan with a blend of fear and confusion.

"Ye actually send people away? Even children?" 'Twas a rhetorical question, his tone filled with revulsion.

One of the women sitting next to Joan decided it might be best to explain the way of things to their addlepated new leader. "'Tis the way of things here," she said. "'Tis nae fair to put a burden on the healthy. If ye cannae help or contribute the rest of the clan, ye *go away*. 'Tis the most righteous thing a person can do for the betterment of the clan."

Aghast, Lachlan, Jamie, and Fergus could only listen incredulously.

"Aye," said the shorter woman. "Every last one of us would do the same. 'Tis a noble sacrifice."

"Noble sacrifice?" Fergus was just as repulsed as his laird and friend were. "Ye call sendin' a little boy away a noble sacrifice?"

Indignantly, Joan sat a little taller in her seat. "Aye, I do!"

"He may never gain use of his arm again," said the other woman. "Ye can see how that could be a burden to the rest of us. Havin' to do his work as well as our own."

"Would it surprise ye to learn that I suffered a similar injury as a lad?" Fergus said, taking a step toward her.

"Ye did?" Mariam said in wide-eyed amazement.

"Aye, I did. I got kicked by a verra angry horse when I was ten. Broke my arm just below my elbow," he said, pointing to his right arm. "I healed and it has never bothered me since."

They all looked at him in awe.

Wanting to put an end to this, Lachlan raised his voice. He wanted to make certain those gathered out of doors heard him as well. "From this day forward, no one, and I do mean *no one* will be sent away for any reason. Nae for a broken bone or an illness or for their age." He shook his head once again. "Do I make myself perfectly clear?"

There were a few who nodded with understanding. The vast majority appeared as though they thought him completely mad. Including the little lad's mum.

"I will nae be held responsible for my son being a burden to anyone."

Realizing there would be no arguing with the woman and worried she might take matters into her own hands and harm the lad, Lachlan went to the bed and scooped the boy up into his arms. "Then ye no longer have a son."

And with that, he stormed out of the cottage and back to the keep.

"THERE IS NAUGHT TO BE DONE FOR HIM, I AM AFRAID." THE healer, or a man who claimed that position, was looking down at little Gylbeart as if the boy had an arrow lodged in his heart. "He is quite doomed."

Lachlan lowered his head and rubbed the space between his eyes with his finger and thumb. "Ye cannae be serious?" He was growing weary of asking that question.

The healer, a short, squat man named Albert, who Lachlan estimated to be near to forty, grabbed up his basket of supplies and tucked it under his arm. "I am. 'Tis broken, just as his mum told ye it was."

"But ye can mend a broken arm," Jamie said.

"To what end?" Albert asked with a scrunched brow. "He will be a burden if it doesn't heal proper."

Thoroughly disgusted, Lachlan looked to Jamie and Fergus. "Remove him from my presence before I gut him."

They were all too happy to do his bidding. Forcefully, they grabbed the man by his upper arms and all but dragged him from the keep.

He was left alone, in a small bedchamber above stairs. Gylbeart appeared both baffled and sad. He lay in the center of a soft bed, the light from the fire in the hearth and candles casting him in shades of gold. A precious, innocent little boy. Lachlan had covered him with a fur and propped a few pillows under his arm earlier.

"I told ye he would nae fix it. 'Tis my own fault for climbin' the tree."

Lachlan sat on the stool by the bed. "Gylbeart, all children climb trees. Some get hurt and that is all right, lad."

He swiped away a tear and shook his head. "I dunnae mind goin' away. 'Tis my duty."

"Yer only duty right now is to get better. And not to worry. We will get that arm of yers fixed and ye will be well soon enough."

"But I dunnae want to be a burden," he replied in a whisper.

Rolling his eyes, Lachlan did his best to reassure the child. "Ye are nae a burden, lad. Nae now, nae ever. I insist ye quit worryin'."

The boy said nothing as he stared at the hearth.

"Lad, when people are sent away, where do they go? Do ye ken?"

Gylbeart nodded as another tear streamed down his cheek. "To the Black Forest. 'Tis haunted, ye ken."

Why anyone would want to terrify a child with being sent to live in a haunted forest was beyond Lachlan's comprehension. Why they would send anyone away was an even greater mystery.

"Does it pain ye much?" he asked.

With a slight shrug, as if to say it mattered not either way, he said, "Only a bit."

Lachlan had a sneaking suspicion the boy was trying to keep a brave face. "Ye are a brave lad, I will give ye that."

Cocking his head to one side, Gylbeart said, "Brave? Me?"

"Ye climbed the tree, nay?"

He nodded in affirmation.

"And I have yet to see ye wail or carry on from the pain," Lachlan said. "Aye, I would call ye verra brave."

THEY CHATTED ON FOR A WHILE, ABOUT INCONSEQUENTIAL THINGS until Jamie and Fergus returned. They had one of the MacDougall men with them.

Thomas the Brown he was called. A tall man with wide shoulders and a beard that very nearly reached his belly. Tucked under one arm was what appeared to be a large leather bedroll. A fur cloak was tied around his neck, making him appear as large as a bear.

His size alone was intimidating. But when he spoke? The deep baritone of his voice was enough to make Lachlan take a step back. "I hear we have a lad with a broken wing?" He grabbed Lachlan's arms and began inspecting them. "I find no broken bones here," he said with a bit of mirth.

Prepared to reprimand the foolish man, he was stopped with a wink and a nod. Jamie stepped forward. "Thomas the Brown is a healer," he explained. "I assumed ye did nae want a Chisolm near the lad after what we learned this day."

Lachlan was in full agreement and thanked Thomas the Brown for coming to their aid.

Thomas looked at the boy in the bed. "I was told there was someone in dire need of healing. But all I see here are hale and hearty men and one wee lad who looks fit and strong."

Gylbeart giggled. "I broke my arm," he said, sounding far more at ease than he had only moments ago.

Glad to see the lad smiling, Lachlan stepped to the opposite side of the bed. "Just a wee broken bone," he informed Thomas the Brown.

"Och! Is that all?" He clucked his tongue and shook his head. "And here I was thinkin' 'twas a man on the verge of death."

Belying his bulk, he was able to sit on the bed without jostling the boy around. "Let us see what we have."

With great gentleness that also belied his bulk and intimidating size, he examined Gylbeart's broken arm. "There is no bone pokin' through the skin."

"Is that good?" Gylbeart asked.

"Aye, it is," Thomas replied. "For if it were, it would be a bloody, ghastly mess and I cannae stand the sight of blood."

Gylbeart scrunched his brow. "I thought ye were a healer?"

"I am," said Thomas. "But I still cannae stand the sight of blood. So for that, I thank ye, young man. Ye have made our jobs much easier."

"Our jobs?"

"Aye, laddie," Thomas said as he placed the leather roll on the bed. In quick order, he had untied the leather bindings and carefully unrolled it, revealing the contents. Small jars and bottles filled with herbs and concoctions. Clean bandages were neatly folded and tucked into pockets. There were sharp knives and other instruments Lachlan didn't recognize.

"Our job," he said giving a slight inclination of his head to the other men in the room, "is to fix that broken arm of yers."

"What's my job?"

"Yer job is to sleep while we do it." He removed two small bottles from the leather satchel. Speaking over his shoulder, he said, "We will need some warm cider and some whisky."

"Ye're going to give the boy whisky?" Jamie asked incredulously

"Of course nae, ye eejit. The whisky is fer us for when we're done."

IT HAD TAKEN NEARLY TWO HOURS TO RESET THE POOR BOY'S ARM. The four men had waited until he was sound asleep before they began their careful work.

"I pray to God that someday, someone invents a way to see inside a body," Thomas said as he pulled on Gylbeart's arm.

Gylbeart groaned, his face twisting in pain, but he was unable to open his eyes. Jamie held a comforting hand on the lad's shoulder while Fergus and Lachlan assisted the healer.

"I also pray we can find better ways of helpin' people without bringin' them more pain or sufferin'."

Once he was satisfied the bones were back in place, he quickly set the arm in a sturdy splint. "When he wakes, he will be in a good measure of pain," he explained.

"Can we give him more of the tincture?" Fergus asked.

"Nay," he replied. "If we give him too much, we risk killin' him. We will have to wait at least eight more hours before we can give him more."

Once his work was done, Thomas stood to his full height and stretched his arms out wide. "I have done all I can for him," he said in a grave tone. "Pray the poor child does nae get a fever."

Fevers, as they all well knew, could be deadly. 'Twas a fever that took Lachlan's mother from him when he was not much older than Gylbeart. A sense of dread fell over his heart.

Thomas withdrew another bottle from his leather roll. "Put a few drops of this into cider every few hours," he said as he placed the bottle on the table next to the bed. "That will help ward off the fever, but 'tis nae a guarantee."

Lachlan and his men stood and stretched, all the while they kept a watchful eye on their patient.

"Why did ye nae call on the Chisolm healer?" Thomas asked as he poured whisky into four mugs. He handed one to each of the men.

Lachlan explained everything they had learned earlier. When he was done recounting the story, Thomas whistled low and shook his head in dismay. "I have ne'er heard the like before," he said. "A bunch of backward eejits if ye ask me."

There was not a man in the room who disagreed.

THOMAS LEFT MORE INSTRUCTIONS BEFORE QUITTING THE ROOM. Jamie and Fergus left with him to see about getting something to eat. Moments after they left, there came a knock upon the door.

Cautiously, as he still hadn't gained the fealty of these people, Lachlan opened the door with his sword drawn.

'Twas Murdoch standing on the other side. He raised one eyebrow when he saw Lachlan's sword at the ready. Raising both hands in the air, he said, "I am unarmed."

"What do ye want?" Lachlan asked gruffly. He was in no mood for nonsense from any of the Chisolms, let alone the man who'd been a thorn in his backside ever since his arrival.

He shifted his weight from one foot to the other. In a low whisper, he asked, "Did ye mean what ye said earlier? About no one bein' sent away again?"

"I say what I mean and I mean what I say," Lachlan told him. "The practice of sending the less fortunate away stopped today."

Murdoch glanced to his left then his right as if he were afraid of being seen talking to the new laird. "What about those who were already sent away?"

Lachlan hadn't had time to consider that. "Come in and let us discuss it."

LACHLAN POURED TWO CUPS OF WHISKY, HANDED ONE TO MURDOCH before taking a seat near the hearth. The two men faced one another and spoke in low tones. Gylbeart slept, albeit peacefully, nearby, and

Lachlan did not wish to wake him. "Tell me about this being sent away nonsense," Lachlan said as he sipped on the whisky.

Murdoch leaned forward in his seat, rolling the mug between his hands. "I am nae sure when it began," he said. "It has been happenin' for as long as I can remember."

"Has it always been this way?"

"Nay," he replied as he took a sip of whisky. "I can remember my grandfather speakin' of the times *before*, as he called them. If I remember what he said correctly, it all began with Maitland's father, Randall the first."

Lachlan leaned forward and listened intently as Murdoch explained things as he knew them to be.

"Somethin' happened long ago betwixt Randall the first and an older member of the clan. What that somethin' was, I dunnae ken. From what grandfather said, 'twas nae long after and the man disappeared. Randall the first told the clan the man went away because he was auld and dinnae want to be a burden. Soon after, Randall started suggestin' that others go away. All for the betterment of the clan."

Lachlan sat in stunned silence, almost mesmerized by the story Murdoch was telling him.

"Before anyone realized it, all sorts of people were bein' sent away for all sorts of reasons. Some went voluntarily, ye ken. But for many, 'twas a not-so-polite *suggestion*. After several years, there remained no elderly, save for my grandfather."

He fell quiet for a long moment, reliving memories only he could see. Lachlan left him to his quiet reverie.

"My grandfather was a strong, braw man. A fine warrior. A man with a good heart." He took a long pull of whisky, draining the mug. "They sent him away because he *might* someday become a burden. But I kent the truth of it."

"And what was the truth of it?"

Murdoch blew out a long, heavy breath. "Because he was the last who remembered the times before. He knew too much."

LACHLAN THOUGHT ABOUT WHAT MURDOCH WAS TELLING HIM.

"Get rid of those who remember so that ye can change yer own history." He shook his head, loathing the thought.

"Aye, now ye have the way of it."

"But how could the people accept this?" For the life of him, he couldn't quite grasp how the people of this clan allowed such a thing to happen.

"Because we were in times of plenty," Murdoch said. "And Randall the first gave one fat sheep and a few chickens to each member of the clan."

"Their fealty was purchased?"

"I suppose it was," Murdoch replied.

Both men fell silent for a long while, each lost in his own thoughts. 'Twas Murdoch who broke the lengthy silence. "They all went to the Black Forest. 'Tis about two miles from here. No one ever ventures there. They avoid it like the plague."

Lachlan nodded his understanding. "That is why they believe it is haunted. All the souls they sent there to perish."

Murdoch rubbed the edge of the mug with his thumb. "I dunnae believe all have perished."

"What makes ye say that?"

"Because I have actually gone there."

WHY DID THIS NOT SURPRISE HIM? MURDOCH HAD PROVEN SINCE the beginning that he was not the sort to just bend to anyone's will. Lachlan was starting to see the man in a slightly new light. Nay, he wasn't ready to put his full faith and trust in him, but mayhap he wasn't quite the bloody bastard he'd thought him to be.

"And what can ye tell me about the Black Forest?" Lachlan asked, his curiosity growing.

"I can tell ye it is nae haunted," Murdoch said with a wry smile.

"I never believed that it was," Lachlan told him. "Am I to assume the ghosts and banshees are those who have survived bein' sent away over the years?"

"Aye, 'tis safe to assume that, laird."

'Twas the first time he'd addressed Lachlan as laird. "Is yer mother one of those survivors?"

Murdoch leaned back in his chair and stretched out his feet. "She is. And she is doin' quite well."

"How many are there?"

"A few dozen," Murdoch answered.

"I want ye to go to the Black Forest and bring yer mother back. And ye let everyone ken they will be welcomed back into the clan. No one, from this day forward, will ever be sent away for any reason other than treason. Ye tell them their new laird has ordered it so."

Just as Lachlan was beginning to see Murdoch in a new light, Murdoch was seeing his new laird quite differently. "As ye wish, laird."

When Murdoch left, Lachlan hoped this was the beginning of something new that would eventually bring this clan together.

"WHAT DO YE MEAN WE OWN A BROTHEL?" LACHLAN ALL BUT shouted the question.

Jamie and Fergus were doing their best not to laugh.

Walter was quaking in his boots. "Just that, laird. The clan owns a brothel."

A deep ache began to form at the base of Lachlan's skull.

"'Tis how the clan has survived most of our lean years, laird," Walter explained. "'Tis quite profitable."

Lachlan's thoughts immediately turned to Keevah. He could not, in good conscience, remain the owner of a brothel, when the woman he loved was a former prostitute. *Lord, what would she think of me?* Nay, he could not allow the clan, whether it be Chisolms or MacCulloughs, to run such a venture.

"Get rid of it," he ground out.

Walter was so astonished that his eyes bulged as his mouth fell open. "Get rid of it?" He stammered.

"Aye," Lachlan said. "We will nae be the owners of any establishment whereby we earn coin off the backs of women."

Walter looked to Jamie and Fergus for help, but they were too busy looking at the floor at their feet.

"But, laird, we cannae do that."

Lachlan scowled. "I believe we have already established the fact that I am laird. My orders are nae to be questioned or contradicted. Is that clear?"

"Aye, laird, 'tis perfectly clear," Walter said.

Satisfied, Lachlan was just about to dismiss the man to do his bidding when he said, "But nae in this particular circumstance."

Frustrated, Lachlan got to his feet. Before he could order the man be hanged for his insolence, Walter began to explain the why of it. "'Twas a gift from David's grandsire."

"David who?" Lachlan asked with a biting edge to his tone.

"King David," Walter said before swallowing hard again. "King David's grandsire, Robert de brus. He gifted what most people call the Tickled Pickle to Randall Chisolm, the first, some fifty years ago."

The ache in Lachlan's skull intensified.

Jamie and Fergus nearly fell to their knees. "The Tickled Pickle?" Jamie asked, gasping for breath.

A tic formed in Lachlan's jaw.

Walter did his best to ignore the two men. "It will be owned by the Chisolms in perpetuity."

"But ye are no longer Chisolms," Jamie pointed out.

"No matter what we call ourselves, the Tickled Pickle will be owned by whomever occupies this keep."

Fergus, always the stalwart and logical thinking of their group, couldn't contain his laughter. His body shook as his eyes watered. Lachlan glared with the intention that his fierce scowl would quiet the man. It had the opposite effect.

"Would ye please stop callin' it that?" Lachlan said to Walter. To his men, he said, "I dunnae ken why ye think this is so amusing."

Neither man could answer, for they could barely catch their breath.

"Laird, as much as I would like to do yer biddin', I cannae do it. 'Tis impossible."

"Nothin' is impossible," Lachlan said derisively.

Walter had to ask him to repeat himself for he couldn't hear over Jamie and Fergus's belly laughs.

"For the love of Christ!" Lachlan shouted. "If ye cannae control yerselves, then leave."

They laughed all the way out of the study. Lachlan waited until the sound of their amusement was nothing more than a faint echo before turning his attention back to Walter.

"If we cannae get rid of it, then shut it down."

Walter's expression changed from nervous to terrified. "I'd rather ye just hang me now, laird," he said. "Fer I would rather that than to go to Inverness and tell Madam Euphemie that she is to shutter her doors."

Back and forth they went for nearly half an hour. Not even the threat of death could get Walter to change his mind.

Realizing he was not going to get the weak man to acquiesce, Lachlan decided all further arguments were unnecessary. While he had absolutely no desire to go to Inverness, he had no other choice.

Chapter Eight

One of the benefits of killing whores is that they made it so damnable easy. One would think that after the brutal deaths of six of their ilk, any whore with half a mind would be a bit more cautious. But nay, they were all far too eager to earn their piece of silver or gold.

He'd been studying his next victim for weeks now. Watching, waiting in the shadows, carefully taking mental notes of where she went and when. Number seven rarely left the confines of the filthy brothel where she lived and worked. Madame Euphemie's. Bah!

No matter what they called it or what kind of expensive and pretty draperies they hung in the windows, no matter the type of clientele who visited - earls, dukes, merchantmen - 'twas still a den of iniquity. A house of ill-repute. A home for whores.

Forveleth.

He only knew her name because he'd heard someone call her that a sennight ago. Whores never paid attention to the shadows, or what lurked within.

If she weren't a whore, he might find her quite becoming, what with her dark hair and big green eyes. He could see why a man might be tempted by such a delight. But he wasn't most men. Nay, he was doing God's work. That set him apart from all other men.

'Twas a chilly Tuesday, late afternoon. Whores slept most of their days away, he supposed.

Forveleth slipped out of the back door of Madame Euphemie's Tickled Pickle - an awful name for a bordello he mused quietly. As she did every Tuesday afternoon, she quickly made her way down the alley and turned left.

He followed behind her, unnoticed by her or anyone else for that matter. He blended seamlessly into the small crowds and other shoppers. No one would look at him and think "There is a man doin' God's work." Or better still, "there is a man who will soon kill someone."

Nay, he fit in quite nicely.

He paused to look at an assortment of bread at the baker's just as Forveleth slipped inside the healer's home. Three doors down from the bakers, 'twas an inconspicuous space but he knew the kind of things that particular healer did. Tending to whores and foul women.

'Twas a giddy sensation knowing that a sennight from now, he'd be running his blade across Forveleth's throat.

And she had no idea she had very little time left to live.

Chapter Nine

The Tickled Pickle was nestled inside a fine building a few blocks east of the River Ness. Three stories tall, made of limestone, there was a fine tavern on one side and a jeweler on the other, and a woolers on the corner.

The Tickled Pickle was run by the world renowned Euphemie Boyer. World renowned for being well-versed in the art of gratifying a man. 'Twas a well-known secret that she was actually the illegitimate daughter of Robert de Brus, the sixth earl of Annandale. Not to be confused with the Robert the Brus, the former king of Scotland. Aye, Euphemie was sister to *that* Robert the Brus, though she'd never had the pleasure of meeting either man in person.

But her mother, Elyne Boyer, was one of Robert de Brus's most favored lemans. So much so, that he gifted her the building that her daughter now resided in, although in a round-about-way.

In order to keep the not-so-well kept secret secret, Robert deeded the land and building to his cousin, Randall Chisolm, the first. Three generations of Chisolms had taken great pride in ownership. 'Twas said that Randall the first often visited the Tickled Pickle. 'Twas also said he had brought his son, Maitland here to get done with the learnin' of bein' a man.

It was also known in the seedier parts of Inverness, that if a woman was in trouble, she could go to Euphemie for help.

And that is just what Kiernan McInnes' friend and neighbor did. 'Twas auld Mrs. MacElany who had discovered Kiernan's near lifeless body, not more than a quarter of an hour after Kiernan's husband finished beating the poor woman.

With the help of her husband, George, Mrs. MacElany loaded Kiernan - battered, bloody, with swollen eyes, lips, and broken bones - and her daughter Brigid, into the back of a wagon and took them straight to Euphemie.

Euphemie knew who Kiernan was. She'd met the lass a few times, years ago, when Keevah lived here. Without asking who had done such a thing to the sweet, pretty lass, Euphemie had one of her hired men, a tall, strapping man named Charles, take the poor woman above stairs, straight to her own bed chamber on the second floor.

'Twas Euphemie who penned the letter to Keevah. She paid an extra ten groats to Charles's younger brother, Drake, to take the message straight away to the MacCullough Keep. *Do nae stop for man nor beast,* Euphemie had ordered him. *And bring Keevah here straight away.*

A healer was sent for and she arrived quickly. One look at the woman and she shook her gray-haired head. "Jesu," she exclaimed. "I will do the best I can."

"Do better than that," Euphemie told her. "She is nae one of us, Lora." As if that mattered one whit to the aulder woman.

Scoffing, she shook her head again. "I care nae who she is, ye ken that, Euphemie," she said as she set her basket of herbs and supplies on the floor near the bed. "Was it her husband who did this?"

"Aye," Euphemie nodded as she sat on the bed next to Kiernan. "I hope he burns in hell someday soon."

Euphemie stayed with the healer for as long as she could. When night fell, she painted on an air of grace and good humor before descending the stairs to greet guests.

This wasn't her first foray into keeping a woman safe from an abusive, ugly husband or lover. She and her ladies had helped a goodly number of women heal or escape over the years and no man was ever the wiser.

Nay, keeping Kiernan's presence here wasn't the problem.

The problem would be keeping her alive until Keevah arrived.

YULETIDE WAS ONLY A FEW WEEKS AWAY. THE MACCULLOUGH women were beginning to ready the keep for the weeks-long celebration. Dried flowers and evergreens were hung from the chandeliers and mantles in the gathering room, adding a most festive air to the keep.

On this cold, snowy afternoon Keevah, Aeschene, and Marisse were gathered near the hearth. While Aeschene and Marisse were in light spirits, the same could not be said for Keevah.

"Ye can never have too many sleeping gowns for yer bairn," Marisse said as she carefully stitched the hem to another gown. The blue fabric was as soft as down and she couldn't resist smiling as she sewed.

Weeks ago, a few of Richard's men had retrieved her loom from her cottage and placed it near the hearth. She'd been working on another blanket for Aeschene's babe, using blue, red, and green yarn. Twice now, she had to stop and redo her work for she had absentmindedly made several of the loops too loose. Her mind was not on her task this day. Instead, 'twas focused entirely on a man who was a two-day ride away. A man who hadn't kept his promise.

"I do thank ye for the blankets," Aeschene said with a nod towards Keevah. "I have never felt anything so soft."

Keevah hadn't been listening. She'd been too busy cursing under her breath for having made yet another mistake in her work.

Marisse leaned over her chair to whisper in Aeschene's ear. "She is nae payin' attention."

Before Aeschene could respond, one of Richard's men came bursting through the door and down the steps. "M'lady! M'lady!"

All three women jumped with a start.

"M'lady," he called out again.

"Good heavens, Henry. Calm down," Marisse admonished. "We are nae deaf."

Out of breath, he stood between Marisse and Aeschene. "I be terribly sorry, but 'tis important." The urgency in his voice was unmistakable.

"Well?" Marisse asked after allowing him time to catch his breath. "What is so important?"

He glanced at Keevah, who had left her place at her loom. "'Tis an urgent missive for Keevah."

Keevah stared at the rolled parchment he held in his hands. She'd never received a missive before. Urgent or otherwise.

A slight blush crept up her neck, flushing her cheeks. She took the scroll into her hands and thanked him.

The young man left as quickly as he'd arrived. Keevah continued to stare at the scroll for several long moments as her heart pounded against her breast. *Mayhap 'tis from Lachlan,* she dared to hope.

"Well?" Marisse asked. "Are ye nae goin' to read it?"

Her blush intensified. "I cannae read."

Marisse rose from her chair and placed a comforting palm on her hands. "Would ye like me to read it for ye?"

Truly, there was no other way around it. No matter who the missive was from, she couldn't have read it there were there a dirk to her throat.

One look into Marisse's eyes and she knew that no matter what message was written, Marisse would not humiliate or embarrass her. "Aye, please."

Gently, Marisse took the parchment from her hands and looked at the seal. "I dunnae recognize the seal," she said.

Neither did Keevah.

Marisse carefully unrolled the document and began reading aloud.

Dear Keevah,

I fear I have the worst of news for ye, lass. 'Tis Kiernan. He has finally done it and we fear she is nae long for this world. She has asked for ye and I believe ye ken why. Come at once.

Euphemie.

KEEVAH'S HEART FELT AS THOUGH IT HAD PLUMMETED TO HER FEET and bounced up again as an intense ache filled her heart. She hadn't heard either name spoken aloud in many years.

"The bloody bastard," she cursed.

AESCHENE AND MARISSE WERE QUIET FOR A LONG WHILE, WAITING patiently for an explanation. Keevah could only stare at the parchment, her mind whirling, her heart breaking.

"Who is Kiernan? Who is Madame Euphemie, and who is *he*?" Marisse asked in a low whisper.

Keevah tamped down her anger and swallowed back her tears. "Kieren was my dearest friend," she began, her throat suddenly feeling quite dry. 'Twas, in fact, an understatement. She and Kieren had been closer than friends. They'd been like sisters. Kieren knew all of Keevah's secrets - secrets she would take to her grave.

"And Madame Euphemie?" Aeschene asked.

Keevah gave a slow shake of her head. "A friend to each of us. And aye, before ye ask, she is that kind of madame."

No further explanation was needed. Both women knew of Keevah's past.

More silence fell as a rush of memories, many good, some not as precious, came rushing into her mind. The ache in her heart continued to intensify.

"And who is he? What does it mean 'he has finally done it?'" Marisse asked.

Keevah swallowed her tears. "Her husband, Dermott," she began as she slowly fell into the chair next to Aeschene. He was one of the most brutal, unforgiving men she'd ever known, and she'd known a lot of men.

She thought back to the last time she'd seen Kiernan. *"He has changed, now that I have given him a child."* Dermott hadn't always been a ruthless bastard. Nay, those changes came long after he and Kiernan were married. Both women believed that once she was able to give him a child, his anger would subside. Apparently, they'd both been wrong.

"She has a daughter," she explained. "Brigid. She is nearing six years old now. "I had believed he had changed, after Kiernan gave him a child. Now, I know I was wrong."

"Och, Keevah," Marisse said as she knelt in front of her. "I am so sorry."

"We will arrange for yer escort to Inverness at once," Aeschene said.

Keevah was wholly surprised by the offer. "But—"

Aeschene would not allow her to protest. "Yer friend needs ye," she said. "Ye must go at once."

Keevah allowed the tears to finally fall, a blend of heartache and relief. "Thank ye," she murmured as she swiped away her tears.

Kieren, please wait for me, she prayed. And *God, please do nae let Dermott find them*.

<hr>

IN LESS THAN TWO HOURS' TIME, KEEVAH HAD PACKED HER belongings, said her goodbyes, and was being escorted through the gates of the MacCullough keep. Eight of Richard's finest warriors had been put in charge of her safety.

Keevah refused to wonder why they had all volunteered for this duty. More likely than not, the young men were simply eager for a chance to be away from the keep, and a chance to find some excitement in Inverness.

She sat atop a fine gray mare and tried to remember the last time she had ridden a horse. It had been years.

The wind was bitingly cold, whipping and thrashing all around them. Thankfully, there was only a light dusting of snow. It would take three days for them to reach Inverness.

As the wind intensified, she pulled her cloak more tightly around her torso. She was very thankful for the warm mittens and fine woolen scarf her friends had gifted to her. Still, she felt cold; cold to her bones.

But she knew 'twasn't the biting wind that chilled her. 'Twas her memories intermingled with guilt.

As they traveled along the winding dirt road, her thoughts kept returning to Kiernan and Brigid. Guilt assaulted her heart and mind. *I should have kept in touch. I should have at least tried to visit. I should have done more. How could we have been so stupid as to believe Dermott had changed?*

Truly, they hadn't possessed many choices. According to the laws of Scotia, Kiernan and Brigid were Dermott's property, to do with as he wished. They could have run away, but chances were good he'd have dragged them back.

"Do ye need to stop, lass?" 'Twas Aric, one of the older men assigned to protect her. He looked genuinely concerned for her.

"Nay," she replied solemnly. She needed to get to Inverness as soon as possible. Before her friend died. Before Dermott discovered where she was hidden. Before he could get to Brigid.

'TWAS THE MIDDLE OF THE NIGHT WHEN KEEVAH AND HER GUARDS arrived in Inverness. Snow fell in soft flakes, leaving a fine dust of snow across the city. Dawn was at least two hours away.

Phillip escorted her to the door and inside the dimly lit space. Years ago, she'd called this place home. A quick glance around the entryway told her naught much had changed.

Pushing through a set of ornately carved doors, she came into the gathering room. The air rushing in fanned the flames of the low burning fire in the hearth to her left. It caressed the flames of the fat beeswax candles scattered around the room. Expensive upholstered chairs and chaises were carefully placed here and there. Tables of varying sizes, covered in silk and lace held those candles.

A moment later, Charles, Euphemie's personal guard, entered from the hallway on the other side. Recognizing Keevah at once, he spun around and left.

"Who is he?" Charles asked.

"Euphemie's personal guard. He is a good man," she answered in a hushed whisper. She went to the fire and rubbed her hands together. Cold to her bones, she shivered as she soaked up the warmth from the fire. Phillip remained quiet and vigilant, maintaining at his post by the double doors.

Moments passed before Euphemie came rushing into the room. As always, she was elegantly dressed in silk and brocade. Her auburn hair was perfectly coiffed with braids twisting around her scalp, the rest cascading down her back in a river of curls.

"Keevah," she said as she rushed to pull her in for a warm embrace. "Thank God ye are here." Immediately, she began pulling her toward the stairs. "She is nae long for this world, Keevah. I think she has been holdin' on just for ye."

Tears stung at her eyes, but she refused to free them. "Where is Brigid?"

"Asleep in Mava's room," she replied. "Dunnae worry over it. Mava is our new cook and housekeeper. She has a room next to the kitchens. Away from everyone."

Relieved the child was in someone's good care, she followed Euphemie up the stairs. "I put her in my room," she said as she led the way down the dimly lit hallway. "Shareen is with her now."

They paused outside the door to Euphemie's room. Euphemie hugged her once again and stepped aside. "Call for me if ye need me lass." She patted her hand and disappeared into the shadows.

KEEVAH TOOK IN A DEEP, STEADYING BREATH BEFORE SLOWLY opening the bedchamber door. The soft light from the hallway spilled in, washing over the bed on the opposite side of the room. The only other light coming from the low-burning fire in the brazier and one lonely beeswax candle that sat on the bedside table. Globs of wax had dripped over the holder and pooled on the tabletop.

There, in the large bed, bathed in half-light, was her friend, Kieren. Barely recognizable now her face covered in dark bruises that were visible even at this distance. Keevah rushed to her side, fell to her knees as she took her hand. "I am here, dear sister. I am here."

Kienan's once beautiful, bright blue eyes were half swollen from the beating her husband had given her. Lips that at one time in her life were so easy to curve into a warm, beaming smile, were now cut and protruding macabrely. With gentle fingertips, Keevah lightly brushed the blond curls away from her forehead only to find a large, bulging cut that someone had stitched back together. Her delicate alabaster skin had turned purple in so many places. *Lord above! She has been here for days. What must she have looked like when she arrived?*

Tears pooled in Keevah's eyes, her words catching on the knot of grief in her throat. "Kieren, 'tis me, Keevah." Gently, she squeezed her friend's hands in hers and clutched them against her heart.

Kieren tried to open her eyes, but the effort was too much. "Sister," she whispered. Her voice was raspy and coarse. Oh, what Keevah would not give to have her friend whole and healthy again, to hear that sweet voice once again alive with laughter or song. To see those eyes twinkle with delight and mirth. To be young again, before the harsh realities of life had taken away their innocence.

"Aye, sister, 'tis me."

"I waited for ye," Kieren said. "I told them I would nae die until I saw ye once again."

"Wheest!" Keevah said. "Ye are nae goin' to die. I simply will nae allow it."

Kieren tried to laugh, but it came out sounding sickly and hoarse. "Still the bossy one. Even after all these years."

A weak smile formed on Keevah's lips. "Aye, and ye must listen to me. Ye will live. I will take ye and Brigid back to my home with me." 'Twas a dream she'd given up on long ago, but one she would give her right eye to have a chance for again.

She shook her head ever so slightly. "I should have listened to ye years ago," Kieren said. Her breaths were growing shallow and ragged. "I fear I am nae long for this world, Keevah."

Keevah didn't want to listen. But deep down she knew her friend was speaking naught but the truth.

"Remember the promise we made to each other all those years ago?"

Keevah knew exactly which promise her friend spoke of. If

anything ever happened to Kieren, Keevah would take Brigid and raise her as her own. "Aye, I do," she answered, choking back tears of anguish and guilt. *If only I had been more persistent, had refused to take no for an answer...*

"Please, take Brigid for me. Dinnae let him have her." Her voice, although weak, was filled with dread and fear. She took in another ragged breath as her skin grew darker. "Please, make this promise to me."

"Of course!" Keevah exclaimed in a whisper. "I promised ye long ago that I would." She hadn't seen Brigid since the day she was born. More painful memories assaulted her heart.

She looked relieved and at peace. "Have ye seen her?"

"Nae, not yet."

"She is such a beautiful little lass. My little lass." Another ragged breath. The conversation was quite literally draining the life from her. "Our little lass."

"Aye, our little lass," Keevah said as she held onto her hand, willing her not to give in, silently begging her to fight to live.

"I can go in peace now, knowin' our little lass will be safe with ye."

Nay! Please, please dinnae go.

"Shed no tears for me, sister. I made my choices just as ye made yers."

How could she not weep for the loss? Kieren's life wasted on a man who could never and would never love her as she deserved. "Love our little lass, Keevah. Love her as I did. Love her better than I did."

She swallowed hard before replying. "I will, Kieren. I promise to never let her forget ye."

Kieren took no more jagged breaths as her skin darkened to an ugly shade of purple before turning gray. 'Twas then, and only then, that Keevah let her tears fall.

LACHLAN ARRIVED AT THE TICKLED PICKLE BEFORE DAWN. HE'D left Jamie and Fergus in charge of the keep. It was simply too dangerous a time to leave anyone else in charge.

Murdoch, much to Lachlan's surprise, insisted on coming with him. After their lengthy conversation regarding sending clanspeople away, Murdoch had privately sworn his fealty. It seems his own mother had been sent away a few years ago, due to ill health. As soon as they returned from Inverness, Murdoch was going to bring his mother home, and anyone else who wanted to come.

Along with them were a dozen faithful warriors - a handful of McDunnahs and more MacCulloughs.

Once Lachlan was finished with the business of getting rid of the brothel, they would immediately return and begin the process of bringing the rest of the Chisolms to heel. Or he'd die trying.

While he doubted anyone was still awake at this hour, he wanted to get the business over with as soon as possible. Besides, if they lingered too long, lord only knew what trouble his men might find to occupy their time.

He ordered his men to wait with the horses as he and Murdoch went to have his formal discussion with Euphemie.

He pounded on the heavy wooden door and was surprised to have it opened almost immediately. Standing on the other side of the door was a large, ferocious looking man. Lachlan estimated him to be near to thirty years old. Long, dark hair was pulled back at his nape. A slight scar could be seen near his forehead. Dark, piercing eyes stared back at them.

"I am Lachlan MacCullough," he said. "I am here to see Euphemie."

"She is busy," the man replied as he tried shutting the door.

"In case word has nae reached ye yet, I am the new laird of the Chisolm clan."

He showed no emotions as he stepped aside and allowed the men entry. He led them through the heavy double doors and into a spacious room. "Wait here," he said before disappearing into the darkness.

BY THE TIME EUPHEMIE APPEARED, THE SNOW HAD MELTED FROM their boots and cloaks, leaving puddles on the floor under their feet.

He heard Murdoch gasp when the woman all but floated into the room. Aye, she was a beautiful woman and not at all what he had been expecting.

Auburn hair, bright green eyes, and an ample bosom. She wore a dark blue silk and brocade gown. Draped over her shoulders was a fur wrap he guessed was made out of ermine.

Everything about the woman belied what he knew about prostitutes.

"Laird," she said, looking directly at Lachlan. "I am Euphemie. I had heard there was a bit of a dust up at the Chisolm keep. I take it ye are the new MacCullough laird?"

"I am," Lachlan said with a slight inclination of his head.

"Congratulations then, to ye. But the hour is late. I fear all our ladies have retired for the night. Perhaps ye could come back later this night."

He resisted the urge to roll his eyes. Murdoch nodded as if he were enchanted and started toward the door.

"I am nae here to seek the comfort of yer ladies," Lachlan told her.

"Oh, I fear we do nae have any young men in residence. Ye would want to visit the Cock and Bull. It is a few blocks down the street."

Either she was intentionally trying to rile him or she was being sincere; he couldn't be certain and neither did he care. "Madam, I am nae here for that either. I am here to discuss the terms of the agreement between the former Chisolm clan chiefs and ye."

"Could this nae wait until a more decent time of day?" she asked right before glancing at the staircase behind her.

"I fear it cannae," he said. "I want this business done as quickly as possible."

"Verra well," she replied. As soon as she sat on the chaise, Lachlan and Murdoch took seats near the hearth.

She smoothed out her skirts before giving her full attention to Lachlan. "Now, what is so important that it cannae wait?"

Lachlan wasn't certain where he should begin. "It has only recently been brought to my attention that the Chisolms own yer establishment."

"They dunnae own it entirely," she replied. "Only a small percentage of it."

Walter hadn't made that distinct clarification, but he supposed, in the end, it didn't matter. "Either way, I would like to somehow stop bein' an owner of any sort."

She studied him closely for a long moment. "Are ye thinkin' of shutterin' our doors?"

"That thought had crossed my mind, aye."

He could see the fire of anger burning in her bright eyes. "Do ye have any idea what would happen to the women who work here?" She gave him no time to respond. "They'd be sent to work in the streets, laird. And the streets of Inverness are a dangerous place to be. Especially these past few months. They'd be forced to work in deplorable conditions. They would barely make enough money to eat let alone to keep from freezing to death. Nay, laird, I will nae allow ye to close us down. I owe it to these women to keep them safe."

He waited until she took a breath before interjecting. "I said it *had* crossed my mind. I did nae say that was what I was goin' to do."

Euphemie's glare dimmed only slightly.

"I am morally opposed to what ye and yer women are forced to do just to survive," he began. "Were it up to me, none of ye would have to do what ye do."

She scoffed at his naïveté. "Ye mean, bring pleasure to men when they cannae find it anywhere else?"

He felt his cheeks grow warm. "Aye. That."

"My mother was a prostitute," she told him. "She was a favorite of Robert de brus."

"I am aware of that," he replied. In his mind, it didn't matter if it was a king or a farmer taking advantage of a woman. It was repugnant just the same.

"My mother took great pride in what she did, laird. There is no shame in it."

He knew they would never agree on the matter. "I am sure she was. But we still need to solve the current predicament."

"And how do ye propose to do that laird?"

"By giving the entire ownership to ye."

She could not have been more stunned. "And what do ye want in return?"

"Nothin'," Lachlan replied. "The entire buildin', the business, it would all belong to ye."

From the way she was looking at him, he knew she didn't entirely believe him. "I want nothin' in return, madam. I want only to be done with this business."

She quirked a pretty brow. "Ye say *this business* as if ye have a mouthful of dung."

"I meant no insult, madam."

Still unconvinced of his sincerity, she maintained her icy glare.

"Murdoch, please leave us."

Thankfully, he did not argue. Lachlan waited until the doors closed behind him before he returned his attention to matters at hand. "Truly, I meant no insult. I have reasons for wantin' to end the previous relationship ye have had with prior lairds."

"I am listenin'."

He let out a heavy breath. "Ye see, I happen to be verra much in love with a woman who used to do what ye do. Years ago, she left that part of her life and has tried to start over. I want her to be my wife, but I fear she still worries overly much about what she used to do."

"Does it bother ye? What she used to do?"

He smiled warmly, "Nay, it does nae bother me. I understood her reasons for doin' it and would never hold it against her."

"But ye see, with that statement alone, it is apparent to me ye do."

Confused, he asked for clarification.

"Laird, ye behave as though she *needs* yer understandin'. I imagine ye even forgave her, aye?"

"Of course, I did."

She gave a slow shake of her head. "She does nae need yer forgiveness. No woman who has ever been forced to do what we do, or any woman who outright chose this way of life, needs a man's forgiveness. Only acceptance. To forgive is to say she has done somethin' wrong when in fact, she has done nothin' wrong. She provided a service, that is all."

He couldn't quite see it in those terms but was willing to try to see her point.

"Would ye feel the need to forgive a woman for bein' a seamstress? A laundress? A weaver or a scullery maid?"

Now, he could see where she was going with her line of thinking.

She caught the realization dawning in his eyes. "Then why would ye feel the need to forgive this woman ye claim to love?"

For a long moment, he mulled it over and over. Mayhap she was right. Keevah had done nothing that hundreds, if not thousands of women had done in the past. Each for her own reasons. Still, he thought there had to be a better way to make a living.

"For some of us, we have no choice but to do what we do. A few have reasons of their own. It might be the desire for independence. The need for excitement. Or they work in establishments such as mine, save up enough coin, to buy a business the rest of the world finds a bit more palatable or respectable."

Truly, he'd never thought of it that way. Never once had he ever paid a woman for her company. There was something that didn't set well in his head or his heart about it. Joining should involve two willing people. Paying for the act made it seem ... less.

"Accept her past, laird. But do nae offer her forgiveness. She does nae need it."

Mayhap that was what Keevah had been trying to tell him all those many weeks ago?

⚜

FOR MORE THAN AN HOUR, KEEVAH STAYED NEXT TO HER FRIEND, never once letting go of her hand. She wept until she could weep no more. In between sobs, she made a hundred different promises and twice as many apologies.

Guilt clung to her like a second skin. How could she not feel responsible? Had she stepped in and told Kieren not to marry Dermott to begin with, both their lives might have been set on entirely different paths. Had she not been so busy with her own life to talk her friend out of marrying him. Had she not been so busy grieving the loss of her family. Had she taken the time to pay attention. If she had just done one single thing differently, her dearest friend may still be alive. If she had spoken up. If she had been there ...

If, if, if... Her life now seemed to be made up of nothing but if's. If her father hadn't died ... if her mother hadn't died ... if her brothers hadn't died.

Her mother used to tell her not to fret over ifs or buts. *'Twill do ye nae good to fret over what cannae be changed.*

Oh, how she wished Lachlan were here. What she would not give to have just a bit of his comfort, his kindness, and friendship. To feel those big strong arms of his wrapped around her. Oh, how she missed him.

Wiping her tears on the sleeve of her dress, she stood and took a long look at her friend. "I am so sorry, Kiernan. I am so verra sorry."

She placed a kiss upon her forehead and quit the room. She was not going to leave the act of bathing Kiernan and preparing her for burial to anyone else. This was the last good thing she could do for her.

Slowly, she closed the door behind her and went below stairs.

Chapter Ten

The slightest breath could have knocked her over.

There, in the greeting room, sat Lachlan MacCullough and he was in a deep conversation with Euphemie.

How did he know she was here? Had Aeschene sent word to him?

As soon as she stepped out of the shadows of the hallway, he stood to his full height. His face bore the oddest of expressions, but she didn't care to take the time to parse it out.

Tears streamed down her cheeks as she rushed into his arms. Thankfully, those arms she'd been dreaming of only moments ago, wrapped around her and held her tightly.

"Wheest, lass, wheest," he whispered against the top of her head.

"She's gone, Lachlan. She's gone," she cried into his chest. Clinging to him, she continued to cry.

A moment passed before she felt Euphemie's warm hands begin to rub her back. "Lass, I am so verra sorry."

Lachlan looked to Euphemie for guidance and answers, for he certainly had none of his own. He had no earthly idea as to why he'd find the woman he loved in a brothel in Inverness in the middle of the night. And he certainly didn't know who 'she' was. He could only surmise she had been someone important to Keevah.

Euphemie whispered answers to his unvoiced questions. "Kiernan. She was Keevah's dearest friend since they were children."

That offered only a partial explanation as to why she was here, of all places. Now, he thought, was not necessarily the right time to ask that particular question.

Admittedly, it felt good to have her in his arms. Even if she was sobbing uncontrollably. He closed his eyes and breathed her in. The faint smell of roses blended with wood smoke and winter.

He decided then that the reasons she was here didn't matter. He also decided he would never let her go.

WHEN SHE FINALLY STOPPED CRYING, EUPHEMIE GUIDED THEM TO the chaise. Lachlan sat beside Keevah with an arm draped around her waist. He wasn't quite ready to relinquish his hold just yet.

"I will get ye some warm cider," Euphemie said before quietly slipping from the room.

Keevah dried her tears on the bit of linen Euphemie tucked into her hand before she left. "'Tis the God's truth I never thought to see ye here, Lachlan. But, Lord above, I am glad ye are."

He chuckled softly. "I can say the same."

Puzzled, she sat up to look at him. "I thought Aeschene had sent word to ye."

He gave a slow shake of his head. "Lass, I had no idea ye were here."

More confusion filled her eyes. "Then why are ye here?"

"That is a verra long story, lass. One I will gladly explain to ye someday. Now, tell me why ye are here."

She dabbed at the corners of her eyes and began to explain, as best she could. "Kiernan was my dearest friend, since we were weans, really. She was the closest thing to a sister I have ever had." She swallowed the tears before going on. "Several years ago, she married a most vile, violent man named Dermott. I did nae realize just how violent he could be until ... Had I known, I would have made her go with me, when I went to live with the MacCulloughs."

Above all things, Lachlan hated men who were cruel to women. Anger began to bubble deep in his gut.

"I received a missive from Euphemie a few days ago. Kiernan had been brought here after Dermott—" she couldn't quite get the words out. It hurt too much to say it aloud. "He killed her, Lachlan. He beat her so badly that she died. I made it just in time to say goodbye."

She fell against his shoulder, struggling with tears and guilt. "I should never have left her. I knew he could be mean. I knew, but I did nothin'."

Gently, he rubbed a hand up and down her back. "Lass, ye cannae blame yerself."

"But had I insisted, truly insisted that she go with me—"

"It would have changed nothin'," he told her. "Men like this Dermott ye speak of? He would have eventually found his way to her."

Keevah refused to give any weight to that statement. "He verra well may have, but ye and the MacCulloughs would have kept her safe. I ken that in my heart."

There would be no arguing that point further, at least not for a while. Lachlan knew she was bereft and grieving. Logic rarely figured into one's mind or heart when a person was suffering so.

Changing the subject for now, he asked, "Why was she brought here? And how did Madam Euphemie know where to find ye?"

"Women know about Euphemie's good heart. She has helped more than one woman escape the horrors of a bad husband." She sniffled and snuggled into his chest. "And she knew how to find me because I used to work here."

⁓ ⁕ ⁓

It took every ounce of energy he had not to react to the news. *Here? Of all places?*

He supposed he should find some comfort in knowing she worked here instead of the dark alleys and dangerous streets. His encounter with Euphemie had been brief. Brief as it was, he felt certain she was a good woman who would protect those who worked for her.

"That surprises ye, aye?" she asked. Afraid to look into his eyes, she remained firmly rooted with her head against his chest.

"Truth be told lass, it does. But it matters not."

He felt her relax against him further. He was truly glad he had come here and for the wise advice Euphemie had given him. Had he not come when he did, then Keevah would be grieving all alone. The thought of her going through this by herself made his heart ache.

"How did ye get here?" Certainly, Richard hadn't allowed her to come all this way alone.

"Aeschene made Richard give me an escort. They are stayin' at an inn down the street."

Although he knew Richard wouldn't have allowed her to come alone, he was still relieved at the news. "My men and I will escort ye away from here."

"I cannae leave just yet," she said. "I must tend to Kiernan's burial first."

While he wanted nothing more than to leave Inverness, he wasn't about to leave her alone. "I understand. But ye look done in, lass. Mayhap ye should rest, just a bit?"

Before she could protest further, Euphemie came into the room. In her hands a silver tray filled with the promised warm cider. She placed it on the table in front of the chaise. "He is right, Keevah. Ye need rest."

When she tried to argue against leaving, Euphemie simply smiled. "Think of Brigid. She will need ye well rested in the hours to come."

"Brigid?" Lachlan asked.

'Twas Euphemie who answered the question. "Kiernan's daughter."

THE MORE HE LEARNED, THE MORE QUESTIONS HE HAD. *The poor woman. Not only is she quite literally beaten to death, she also leaves behind a daughter.*

"I will be takin' her with me," Keevah told him as she sat up. She was staring at the crackling fire in the hearth.

He almost asked about the child's father, then realized the idea of turning the child over to such a vile man was repugnant. Even if there were other family members who could or would take the child in, she was undoubtedly safer with Keevah.

There were dark circles under her red, puffy eyes. Quietly, he wondered when she had last ate or slept. The sheer determination in her countenance told him there would be no arguing with her on the matter of Brigid. The only thing he would argue was that she would not be going home with Keevah. She'd be going home with them. He'd explain the rightness of it later, after she'd had a hot bath, a hearty meal, and a good deal of sleep.

"We will keep the child safe," he told her as he took her hand in his. "No matter what." 'Twasn't a promise lightly made. He meant every word of it.

Her shoulders relaxed ever so slightly. Finally, she turned to look into his eyes. "If he could kill his own wife, I doubt he would draw the line at killing her daughter."

She'd gain no argument from Lachlan.

Euphemie cleared her throat to garner their attention. "I think ye and Brigid would be safer here," she told them. "Dermott could verra well be lookin' for Kiernan and Brigid now. I suspect he would look at the inns first."

Lachlan wasn't certain the Tickled Pickle was the best place for a child, however he knew there was merit in what Euphemie was saying. "I have men with me," he said as he stood up. "I will have them stay at the inn down the street. I will stay here with Keevah and the child."

Euphemie tilted her head ever so slightly. "Forgive me, but I am surprised ye would agree."

Keevah was just as surprised as her old friend.

He shrugged his shoulders. "Even I can see the rightness in it. We must protect the child at all costs. Besides, we will only be here until Kiernan is properly seen to."

"I have a large space in the attics," she informed him. "We have hidden people there before."

He gave a short bow at the waist. "Thank ye, Madam Euphemie. Keevah and I will be forever in yer debt."

Dawn was just breaking by the time he finished updating his men and giving them instructions. They would stay at the inn on the corner until after the burial of Kiernan MacInnes.

"Are ye certain ye dunnae wish for at least one of us to stay with ye?" Murdoch asked. There was no underlying mischievousness to his tone. "Ye may need someone to help if the son of whore comes here."

Lachlan thought of Euphemie's guard, Charles. His first duty would be to protect Euphemie. It certainly wouldn't hurt to have an extra hand, just in case. While he knew without a doubt he could defend himself against Dermott, it would be beneficial to have an extra set of eyes.

"Verra well," Lachlan said. "Andrew," he called out to the oldest MacDougall warrior. "Ye will be in charge of keepin' the men out of trouble. I want everyone to rest, nae chasin' bar wenches. Understood?"

Andrew gave a nod of his blonde head before taking his mount's reins. He led the rest of the men down the street in search of stables and beds.

Murdoch followed Lachlan inside and up the stairs to the attics. He knocked once and waited for permission to enter. He didn't want to catch Keevah unaware. He was met with silence. Assuming she had fallen asleep, he slowly opened the door.

They had to duck low to enter. There were two small beds that sat on either side of the sloped ceiling. One window, covered with fur, was straight ahead. A small table sat beneath it holding one burning candle.

Keevah was on the bed to his right with her back to him. He could see nothing else in the dim lighting, so he went to her to pull the covers over her shoulders.

To say he was stunned was a tremendous understatement.

Lying next to Keevah was a black-haired little girl with cherubic cheeks and sooty lashes. Even fast asleep and in the dim light of a low flickering candle, he knew this child could belong to only one woman; Keevah.

She was the spitting image of the woman lying next to her.

What other secrets do ye have? he mused as he looked from the child to Keevah and back again.

What other secrets?

⁂

BRIGID WOKE A FEW HOURS PAST DAWN. CONFUSED BECAUSE SHE didn't know where she was, she sat up and looked around the room and began to cry sleepily. "Mum? Mum, where are ye?" When she received no immediate response, her crying increased.

Keevah sat up with a start and pulled the child to her breast. "Wheest, child, wheest."

"I want my mum," she cried.

"I ken, lass, I ken."

Sobbing now, she continued to ask where her mother was. Keevah felt as though her heart was being ripped from her chest. "Brigid, my name is Keevah," she said in a soothing tone.

Brigid sniffled and pulled away to look at her. "Mum told me about ye," she said. "Ye're my mum's friend."

"Aye, lass, I am," she smiled warmly at her.

"Where is mum?"

Keevah took in a slow, steadying breath, searching for the right words. How does one explain such a thing as a mother dying to a child so young? As she struggled for the words, she felt Lachlan sit on the edge of the bed beside her. He placed a comforting hand on her shoulder. There was such warmth in his eyes that it was nearly her undoing.

"Brigid, yer mum has gone to heaven," Keevah told her.

"Why did she nae take me?" she asked, worry filling her eyes.

Keevah swallowed back her tears. "When people die and go to heaven, they have to go alone."

"Mum died?" she cried, her eyes growing wide. "Like her mum did?"

Keevah nodded, trying valiantly to hold back the tears.

"But mum promised she wouldn't die. She promised!"

Keevah pulled her back in to hold her again. There was naught she could do but hold her and try to comfort her.

"Ye will see yer mum again, someday," Lachlan told her. "But for now, yer mum has asked Keevah and I to take care of ye."

The girl turned her head to peek at him. "Who are ye?"

"I am Lachlan MacCullough," he told her.

"I dunnae ken ye," she said. "I am nae to speak to strangers."

Lachlan smiled fondly at her. "That is a verra good rule to follow," he said. "But I am nae a stranger. I am a verra good friend of Keevah's."

There came a knock upon the door and Murdoch went to answer it. 'Twas Euphemie.

"Keevah, we have moved her to the kitchens," she said from the doorway.

When Keevah tried to stand to leave, Brigid began wailing again. She didn't want to be left with the two strange men. She wanted her mum or Keevah and no one else.

"Brigid, let us break our fast while Keevah tends to something important below stairs. I promise ye, Keevah will come back, lass."

It took a bit of prodding before she would relinquish her tight hold on Keevah. Lachlan scooped her up and stood to his full height. "We need ye to be a strong lass right now, Brigid. Keevah will be back verra soon."

Keevah hurried out the door, leaving one determined Highlander with one equally determined little girl; he intent on keeping her hidden in the attic while she was wholly intent on escaping his clutches.

In the end, he won. With Murdoch's help they were able to get the lass calmed down by allowing her to hold a dirk. Murdoch would have let her kick him in the shin if it meant she'd quiet down. 'Twas an utter heartache to see her so distressed.

"THREE DAYS?" LACHLAN ASKED INCREDULOUSLY.

Keevah could only sigh and shake her head. "The grave digger says the ground is frozen solid. He cannae bury her until it thaws. He thinks the weather will warm in a few days."

'Twas just around noonin' time when Keevah had returned with the news.

News Lachlan was not thrilled with. "He 'thinks'? Lass, I cannae afford to remain here much longer. I have been away from my duties too long as it is."

Brigid had taken a liking to Murdoch, for reasons none of them could understand. Sensing the discussion might get a bit heated, he suggested he and Brigid go below stairs in search of a sweet tart or a bit of bread and honey. She readily and happily agreed.

They waited until the door closed before returning to their discussion. Keevah wrapped her arms around her waist and quirked a pretty brow. Lachlan could see she was angry. "I have nae asked ye to stay, Lachlan. Ye can be on yer way now and back to yer new life. Brigid and I will be fine."

He hadn't meant to upset her. "Keevah, I will nae leave Inverness without ye or Brigid."

"And I will nae leave until I have seen to it that my friend has been properly buried."

"I made a promise to protect ye, both of ye."

"I did nae ask ye to make such a promise. I am perfectly capable of taking care of myself."

"Like Kiernan did?" he chided.

"She was nae strong like me," Keevah seethed. Her green eyes grew dark with fury. "She was far too tender-hearted."

He was about to respond when they heard the most terrifying shriek coming from out of doors. Withdrawing his sword, he went to the window, drew back the fur, and peered out the window. The horrified screaming, continued.

"Stay here," he ordered Keevah.

She wasn't about to listen.

Chapter Eleven

Upon hearing the screaming, Murdoch had handed Brigid off to Euphemie just as Lachlan and Keevah were racing down the stairs.

"It is comin' from the back," Murdoch said.

"We heard," Lachlan said as he searched for a way out.

"This way," Keevah said as she raced past the two men. "The door to the alley is off the kitchen."

She was out the door before he could tell her to remain inside. He had to pull to an abrupt stop so as not to knock her down; she had stopped just outside the door and was staring at something at the end of the alley.

A small crowd was beginning to form toward the end, hovering over something. An older woman was weeping into the chest of a younger woman.

Keevah grabbed a fistful of skirts and ran. Lachlan and Murdoch were fast on her heels. When she reached the huddled crowd, she pushed her way through.

Horrified, her hand flew to her mouth to stop her own scream from escaping.

"Forveleth!" Keevah whispered, appalled at what she was seeing.

Her beautiful auburn hair spilled across the muddy snow. Pretty blue eyes stared up at the gray sky, unseeing, unblinking, lifeless. A large, jagged gash tore across her neck, gaping and bloody.

The top of her dress had been torn, exposing one breast. The skirts of her pretty goldenrod gown had been shoved up to her waist. Her legs had been spread in a most undignified manner.

Keevah's world began to spin as bile rose. The sight of the poor woman, dead, lying in the muddy, icy alley, was worse than any nightmare she could have conjured. 'Twas inhuman, what had been done to her.

Turning away, she found Lachlan standing right behind her. Tears fell as she collapsed against his chest.

"Murdoch, get somethin' to cover the poor lass with," he said, tearing his gaze away from the body.

"Did ye ken her?" Lachlan asked as he pulled Keevah back from the crowd.

She nodded against his chest. "Aye. Her name is Forveleth. Forveleth Boyle."

Lachlan had seen plenty of dead people in his life. Most of them killed on the battlefield. But he'd never seen anything like this. Anger churned deep in his belly. *Who could have done such a thing?*

He'd asked that question too many times of late. Far too many.

Murdoch returned and carefully covered Forveleth's remains. The crowd had grown larger, the murmurs and cruel comments increasing. "Has anyone called the sheriff?" he asked to no one in particular.

No one answered. "I said, has anyone called the sheriff?" he asked again, this time putting a bit of heat and more volume to his inquiry.

A younger man, mayhap in his early twenties, finally tore his gaze away from Forveleth's cold body. "I will," he volunteered before running away.

"Keevah, mayhap ye should go back inside," Lachlan suggested.

"We should nae leave her alone," she replied. Taking a deep breath, she broke the embrace and tried pulling herself together.

"Who would do such a thing?" she asked bitingly, glancing back to Forveleth's linen covered body.

Lachlan had no good answer.

"Only a madman could do that to a woman," Keevah said.

More people were beginning to join the crowd. A sensation began to creep up from Keevah's soul. Vengeance? Fury? Something else? Whatever it was, she was suddenly filled with a tremendous sense of determination.

While she couldn't call Forveleth a close friend, they had spent much time together while working for Euphemie. Searching the crowd, she found the woman she believed had discovered Forveleth's body. She was sitting on a short stool near one of rear doors. She was crying into her skirt whilst the same woman from earlier kept patting her shoulder.

Leaving Lachlan behind, she went to speak to her.

She knelt in front of the poor woman and placed a warm palm on her knee. "Mistress? My name is Keevah. Are ye well?"

She shook her head and continued to quietly weep. "Well? I will never be well again," she cried.

"Neither will I," said the woman beside her. Glancing toward Forveleth, she shivered.

"Were ye the one who discovered Forveleth?" Keevah asked her.

"'Twas Lena who found her," the standing woman said.

Keevah thanked her for that information. "Lena? Can ye tell me exactly what happened?"

She wiped her face with the hem of her skirt before taking in a deep breath. "I opened the door to toss the scraps and there she was. Lying in the mud and snow. The poor woman!"

Trying to keep her voice as calm and warm as possible, Keevah continued with her questions. "Did ye see anyone else in the alley? Anyone lurkin' nearby?"

Lena swallowed hard as she shook her head.

Keevah was looking for anything that might lead to the person responsible for her old friend's death. "Did ye hear anything odd this morn? Anythin' out of the ordinary?"

Another shake of her head.

"I did," said Lena's friend. "I heard a bit of a crash, like someone bumpin' into the crates, less than a quarter of an hour before Lena started screamin'."

"Did ye by chance look to see what it was that was bumpin' around?"

She shrugged her shoulders. "At this hour? I assumed 'twas a drunkard or someone leavin' the Pickle."

Further questioning led to nothing. They saw no one lurking in the shadows, no one leaving the scene of the murder.

Keevah thanked the women and got to her feet. Once again, Lachlan was right behind her, offering her his quiet strength and support.

"What are ye doin', lass?" he asked in a low tone.

She wasn't quite certain what she would call what she was doing or about to do. "I dunnae ken, but I feel I must do somethin' to find the man who murdered Forveleth."

Chapter Twelve

"Are ye mad?" Lachlan asked.

Thrusting her hands onto her hips, she said, "Nay. But I am bloody furious."

"Be that as it may, lass, ye cannae truly expect to go lookin' for a madman. If he would do that," he inclined his head toward Forveleth, "what think ye he would do to ye?"

"I am nae worried about that," she told him bluntly.

His eyes grew wide and his mouth fell open. "Ye are nae worried?"

"Of course, nae. Because ye are goin' to help me."

Murdoch joined them, eager to divulge what he'd learned from members of the crowd. Ignoring his laird's astonished expression and Keevah's determined one, he said, "I was just talkin' to a few people in the crowd. They say this is the seventh woman killed in the past four months."

Keevah and Lachlan turned to him, raised brows and mouths agape.

"Seventh?" Lachlan was beyond incredulous.

"Aye," Murdoch said. "All whores, from what I am learnin'."

"Do nae use that expression," Lachlan warned him.

Murdoch cocked his head slightly. "What are we supposed to call them?"

"Women," Keevah replied sternly. The fire in her eyes warned him not to argue.

Although he didn't quite understand what difference it made, he acquiesced out of respect. "Verra well, m'lady."

Just then a rather loud voice broke over the din of the crowd. "Be gone with ye," the man shouted. "There be naught to see here."

Curious, Keevah walked back to the entrance of the alley.

"I said be gone with ye," he shouted again.

'Twas a man of average height and build, with a bit of a belly protruding from his open wool cloak. His brown trews looked a bit small for a man of his size. Dark of hair, blue eyes, and a full beard, he held an air of either confidence or arrogance. She wasn't sure yet which of the two it was.

"I said be gone," he groused as he looked at Keevah.

'Twas arrogance.

"Why are ye dispersin' the crowd?" she asked. "Should ye nae question them?"

From his expression, he found her revolting. "I am the sheriff," he told her, pulling back his shoulders. "I said leave or ye will find yerself in gaol."

Keevah ignored him. "She was my friend," she told him. "I would like to help in any way I can."

"Ye be a whore then?" He spit on the ground.

Unbothered, for she'd been called far worse, she asked, "What does it matter? She was still my friend. Her name was Forveleth Boyle."

Lachlan placed a hand on the small of her back. "Mayhap we should do as the sheriff requested."

"He did nae make a request; he gave an order. And I refuse to abide it."

He rolled his eyes heavenward and prayed for enough patience to get him through what he was quite certain would be an ugly situation.

"Fancy yerself a bit of time in my gaol, do ye?" the sheriff asked as he glowered at her.

"Of course, nae. I want only to help."

He looked at Lachlan. "Ye best get yer whore under control, laddie, elst I will toss ye both into gaol and throw away the key."

He'd barely finished his sentence when Lachlan was upon him. He grabbed the sheriff by his tunic and lifted him off the ground. "Ye will apologize to my fianceé and I advise ye never to take that tone with her again."

"Who the bloody hell do ye think ye are?" the sheriff asked angrily.

"Lachlan MacCullough."

APPARENTLY, THE NAME MEANT NOTHING TO THE SHERIFF. HE continued to shout to be released and began calling out for his deputies. Only one came running to his aid.

He took one look at the verra angry Lachlan MacCullough and stopped dead in his tracks. Withdrawing his sword, he pointed it at Lachlan's throat. "Ye might want to put the good sheriff MacHenry down."

Murdoch came up from behind the deputy and put the tip of his sword against the man's throat. "Be verra careful what ye do next, laddie. Give it a good measure of thought."

Keevah had had enough. "Of for heaven's sake!" she exclaimed loudly. "Can we end this pissin' contest and focus on the matter at hand? A young woman lies dead at yer feet and all the four of ye can think of is who will kill the other first."

"But he insulted ye," Lachlan reminded her.

"I have been called far worse," she told him. "Now, please, put the man down and let us get on with findin' out who killed Forveleth."

The sound of the name changed the deputy's countenance entirely. His skin turned ashen before he knelt down next to the body. Slowly, he pulled back the linen. For a moment, Keevah believed he might faint. "Forveleth." He shook his head and closed his eyes.

"Ye knew her?" Keevah asked.

"Aye. She was a friend."

"Bah!" the sheriff interjected. "She was naught but a whore just like all the others. Now arrest this man and throw him in gaol!"

As the deputy stood, Keevah felt a flicker of recognition. Had she seen the man before?

"Ye may want to reconsider that, Sheriff. If he is the Lachlan MacCullough I believe him to be, he is one of the king's favored cousins."

'Twas a lie, of course. But only four of the five people present knew it. And just why he'd told it, only he knew.

Lachlan, going along with the deception, cocked his head and smiled at the sheriff. "Aye, 'tis true. Now, apologize to my fiancé."

Stunned, with bulging eyes, the sheriff stammered before he was finally able to get the words out. "I am sorry, m'lady."

Satisfied, Lachlan set the man back on his feet. Smoothing out the man's cape, he patted his chest. "Now, that was nae so hard, was it?"

Believing 'twas a rhetorical question, Sheriff MacHenry decided not to respond. Clearing his throat, he turned his attention to his deputy. "Ewan, ye stay with the who-" he corrected himself with a glance toward Lachlan. "Stay with the body. I will send Coll and Mungo to ye."

He said nothing else before scurrying away like a fat rat who had just escaped death.

"He is the most worthless man I have ever met," Ewan said to no one in particular. "And an even more worthless sheriff."

Lachlan thanked the man, then introduced Keevah and Murdoch. "We thank ye kindly for yer help," he said.

"I be Ewan Holmes," he replied, inclining his head respectfully to Keevah. "Ye and I have met before," he told her. "Years ago. We were but children then. I was friends with yer brothers."

Relieved it wasn't from her time at the Pickled Tickle, her shoulders relaxed. "Och! Ewan!"

"Brothers?" Lachlan asked her. *How many more secrets will I uncover?*

Turning to him she said, "Aye. I had three younger brothers. Unfortunately, the ague took them seven years ago."

He was genuinely hurt for her. He knew what it was like to lose a sibling. Claire, his young sister, died when she was just seven years old, to the same affliction. "I be terribly sorry, lass."

She offered him a warm smile before turning back to Ewan. "Ye knew Forveleth?"

Nodding, he turned his attention back to the deceased. Kneeling down, he pulled the sheet back and looked. Rage filled his gut. "Just like the others," he whispered.

"Others?" Keevah asked as she too knelt down.

"Aye. Seven. All found in back alleys and lookin' verra much like this," he replied without thinking. "Throats cut, skirts pulled up, their-" He immediately stopped himself. "I be so sorry, Keevah. I should nae be talkin' to ye about this." He got to his feet as Lachlan helped Keevah to hers.

"Why nae?" she asked.

"Well, because ye're a woman."

Truly, she wasn't insulted. Still, it did grate. "Be that as it may, I want to help."

"But," he tried choosing his words carefully, "but ye're a woman."

"Ye will find she is a most stubborn woman at that," Lachlan said. "But she is also the strongest woman I ken."

She thanked him kindly for his compliment.

"I did nae say I liked it," Lachlan said drolly.

Ignoring him, she turned back to Ewan. "Is there a madman on the loose?" she asked.

"The sheriff refuses to think so. He tells anyone who asks that the deaths are unrelated."

"But ye think otherwise?" Murdoch asked.

"Aye, I do. Ye cannae tell me that seven different men killed seven different women the same way, and disposed of their bodies in the exact same manner."

"Disposed?" Keevah asked curiously.

"Aye," he said as he knelt down again. "See? With her throat cut like this, there should be more blood here. But there is none." He shook his head once again, made the sign of the cross, and pulled the linen over her.

"I did nae notice that," Keevah told him.

"Have ye anyone ye suspect?" Murdoch asked.

Ewan smiled wanly. "I have an entire city filled with suspects."

"But ye have no clear idea who it is?" Murdoch asked.

Lachlan was growing weary of the conversation. Even Murdoch was being pulled into the mystery. "I am sure Ewan will solve it soon enough," he said. "But as for us, we really should be leavin'."

Keevah looked as though he'd just slapped her. "I told ye I would nae leave until we saw Kiernan properly buried."

"It could be spring before the ground is thawed enough," Lachlan told her.

"Then I shall wait."

He took in a deep breath. "What if we take her with us?" he suggested. "We could bury her on our lands as soon as spring thaws."

"And leave her body to rot in the meantime?" she shook her head. "Nay, I will nae do that to her."

"We have caves where we keep the dead," he politely informed her. "'Tis nae like I want to keep her in the kitchens."

'Twas Murdoch who interjected. "Laird, methinks this might be a conversation best held in private." He gave a nod toward the back door of the Tickled Pickle. Euphemie and Charles were watching closely. Lord only knew who else was paying attention.

"Brigid needs ye," Lachlan said.

She couldn't begin to explain to him *why* she felt the burning need to stay. Keevah wanted to help, in any way she could, to find the madman who had killed her friend.

Any conversations involving Brigid and their future were better done in private. She calmed herself before stepping away and disappearing into the Tickled Pickle.

"What can we do to help?" Murdoch asked.

"What do ye mean, what can 'we' do to help?" Lachlan asked. "We have to get back to the keep."

"I would like to stay and help," Murdoch told him. "I mean, someone is killin' women, Lachlan. The sheriff has no interest in stoppin' the man responsible. Ewan needs our help."

Keevah's curiosity had rubbed off on the man. "Might I remind ye that ye have duties back home?" Lachlan asked as he crossed his arms over his chest.

"But this is far more interestin'," he replied with a wry smile.

"Might I remind ye that yer mum awaits yer return?"

Unmoved, he replied, "'Tis only a few days, Lachlan. I promise I will return to ye in a week. No more than two."

Fully prepared to argue it further, Lachlan was interrupted by the sound of Keevah's voice. He turned to see her coming down the alley. She'd put on her cloak and over one arm carried Lachlan and Murdoch's.

"I thought ye were tendin' to Brigid?" Lachlan said.

"Brigid in is Euphemie's good care," she informed him curtly. "I want to help Ewan."

They'd both gone undeniably mad.

"Truth be told, Laird MacCullough, I could use the help," Ewan said with a most hopeful tone.

Deciding that arguing with either Keevah or Murdoch would get him nowhere, he angrily took the cloak from her outstretched hand. "I will give ye three days, and nae more," he told the three of them. "And I mean nae more."

WHILE THEY WAITED FOR THE GRAVEDIGGERS TO ARRIVE, EWAN continued filling in what he knew about the previous murders. At first, Lachlan was impatient and found it all as interesting as watching a slug crawl across the garden. But by the time Ewan was finished, Lachlan found himself just as intrigued as the others.

Soon, two men approached and gave a greeting to Ewan. "Where is Coll?" Ewan asked.

"Sleepin' off a drunk, I reckon," the very large man answered.

Ewan turned back to the others. "Trevor be the short one, Mongo the larger."

Each man was dressed in black trews and tunics, with dark woolen capes draped over their shoulders.

That was where the similarities ended. Where Trevor was a thin as a willow branch, with a full head of curly blond hair and a long beard to match, Mungo ... well ... Mungo had to have been the largest man Lachlan had ever seen. At least six foot six, he was as broad as a barn.

But not an ounce of fat anywhere. Sunlight glinted off his bald head. A dark red beard fell to his waist, braided in places with little bits of silver jewelry threaded within it.

If he'd come across the man on a field of battle, Lachlan would have retreated.

They carefully placed Forveleth on a wooden stretcher and carried her away.

"Where are they takin' her?" Keevah asked with a good deal of worry.

"To the Black Friars," Ewan replied. "No one else will let prostitutes be buried in their cemeteries." He sounded thoroughly disgusted. "Dunnae worry over it, Keevah. They will take good care of her."

They watched in silence as the men carried their precious bundle down the street and turn the corner.

"It is awfully cold out here," Ewan said. "I have a room just down the road a bit. We can talk more there."

As they were all eager to be out of the cold, they followed closely behind Ewan.

"Are ye certain Brigid is well?" Lachlan asked. He was sincerely concerned for the child's welfare.

"Aye, she is. I promised to be back for the noonin' meal," she told him.

They walked the rest of the way in silence, each lost in their own thoughts. In the middle of the next block, Ewan led them down an alley and turned left. They took a set of wooden stairs to the second floor. He opened the door and took them down a dark hallway. Out of habit, Lachlan's immediately put his hand on the hilt of the dirk in his belt and placed the other on the small of Keevah's back.

They paused halfway down and waited for Ewan to unlock the door. Lachlan glanced both ways before following Murdoch and Keevah inside.

'Twas by no means a spacious or opulently appointed space. Low ceilings overhead made it feel even smaller. A bed was tucked in one corner, with a small table beside it. Along the opposite wall was a long table filled with all manner of documents, books, and parchments.

What truly interested Lachlan was the wall to his left. A large map of Inverness had been carefully painted onto it. Each of the streets carefully labeled in blue paint. Important buildings and points of interest had also been just as attentively applied.

Murdoch whistled as he studied the map. "Who did this?"

"I did," Ewan replied as he hung his cloak on the peg by the door. Immediately, he went to the long table and began scouring through the scrolls and other documents. Finding the one he was searching for, he began reading aloud.

"The first victim was found in the late morning hours on the twelfth day of September. Alisia MacGee. Aged seven and thirty. Blond hair, blue eyes, quite comely for her age. Husband is one Alexander MacGee." Going to the map, he pointed to a little red dot and tapped the area with his index finger. "She was found here, in an alleyway on Kenneth Street."

Turning back to his document. "The next victim was Georgette MacAulay, aged one and thirty. Married to William MacAulay, one son, aged thirteen. She was found in the late morning hours on the second of October on Greig Street." He pointed to another red dot.

"Eighteenth of October, again, late morning hours, the body of Mary Williams was found near Castle Street. Aged two and forty, married to Connor Williams, one child, a daughter, aged nine and ten. On the first of November, Celeste McCreery was found in an alley a block from Mary Williams." The longer he spoke, the more intense he became, pacing back and forth, reading from his scroll, pointing to the map.

"The twenty-first of November, Deirdre Boyden, widowed, one child, a boy, aged seven. Third of December, Mary Andrews, aged seven and twenty, unmarried, one child, aged eleven, a girl. And today, the eighth of December, Forveleth."

He stared at the map as if it held the secrets he needed to find the answers he sought. "Each woman was found in the early morning hours, in alleys around the city. Each had their throats cut, dresses torn, skirts yanked up. There was very little blood at any of the scenes. And no witnesses."

Keevah stepped up to look at the map more closely. A shiver traced up and down her sign. "I knew all but two of the women," she whispered. *There but for the grace of God go I.* "They were all prostitutes," she said.

"*Former* prostitutes," Ewan said. "They were either married now or widowed. One, Mary Andrews, had opened a little seamstress shop about eight months ago."

Keevah listened intently as she tried to make sense of it all.

"I feel as though he is tryin' to send a message," Ewan said. "But what that message is, I dunnae ken."

"He hates prostitutes," Lachlan said, breaking his silence.

"If that were the case, why is he killin' former prostitutes?" Murdoch asked. "Why nae those who are still whor- in that line of work?"

"There is more, something I have nae shared with the Sheriff or anyone else," Ewan said as he returned to his table. "At each of the sites, a small wooden crucifix was left behind."

He opened a small wooden box and retrieved one of the crucifixes. 'Twas crude craftsmanship at best. He handed it to Lachlan for his perusal.

"Tis naught more than pieces of rushes tied together with a bit of coarse wool," he said after looking at it for a quick moment.

"Aye, they are. One was left, either on, next to, or verra near each of the victims."

"Did ye find one with Forveleth?" Keevah asked.

He nodded and pulled the small crucifix from the pouch on his belt. It looked like the others. Bits of twisted brown grass tied together with a bit of coarse woolen thread.

They were all quiet for a long moment.

"And there is nae a witness to be found anywhere?"

"None that I have come across. But the sheriff will nae allow me to question the people who live or work in those areas where they were found."

"Why the bloody hell not?" Lachlan asked bewilderedly.

"Because he is as worthless as a sheriff as he is a man. He is too busy tryin' to impress the aristocracy. A murdered prostitute is simply a murdered prostitute."

"I wager is this madman was killin' the daughters of the aristocracy the sheriff would have a much different opinion," Keevah said frustratedly.

There was not one of among them who would argue that point.

FOR THE NEXT HOUR, THEY DISCUSSED EVERYTHING EWAN KNEW about the murders. The main commonalities as well as the differences. All the while, Ewan paced from the map to his table and often would think aloud.

An ache was beginning to form in Keevah's neck; literally and figuratively. The lack of sleep was catching up with her, but she wanted to press on.

"So, what we do know is that all these women are former prostitutes. Each of them had at least one child. And the murderer leaves behind a crucifix made from rushes."

"Only six of the seven had children," Ewan corrected her. "Celeste was the only one without a child. Celeste had no children."

Keevah shook her head. "I knew Celeste. She did have a child. A little girl. She would have been eleven or twelve had she lived."

Surprised, Ewan went back to his table and riffled through his papers. "I did nae find that information," he mumbled to himself.

Lachlan had been watching her closely for a long while. Something began to gnaw at his gut. *Keevah could have been one of these women.* The thought was terrifying to him. Even though they had yet to have the discussion regarding Brigid, he knew, deep down, the child had to be hers.

"Did ye ken *all* of these women?" he asked her.

"I knew five of them," she replied.

The overwhelming urge to grab her and take her as far away from Inverness washed over him. He didn't want her in the same city as this madman.

"I think we should get back to Brigid," Lachlan told her. "I did nae get to break my fast this morn."

"I think ye are right," she said as she got to her feet. Lachlan grabbed their cloaks from the peg and draped hers over her shoulders.

"I think I would like to stay and talk with Ewan," Murdoch said from his seat near the brazier.

While Lachlan would have preferred Murdoch to help assist with guarding Keevah and Brigid, he decided to allow it. "Verra well," he said. "Please let us know if ye discover anythin' else."

They said their goodbyes and quit the room.

The walk back to the Tickled Pickle seemed to take far too long. Lachlan remained diligent, scanning the area for anyone who might appear as if they wanted to do them harm. Not only did he now need to protect Keevah and Brigid from Dermott, he felt he now needed to protect her from a deranged murderer.

"When we get back to Euphemie's, I want ye to promise me ye will rest. At least for a little while."

"I will nae argue with ye," she said with a smile. "I am exhausted."

Glad to hear her agree, he picked up the pace. He never thought he'd be so happy to walk through the doors of a brothel in his life.

USING THE BACK STREETS AND ALLEYWAYS IN ORDER NOT TO BE SEEN felt odd to Keevah. Until the day she'd left all those years ago, she'd never been afraid to show her face in public. Not even after she started working at the Tickled Pickle.

"We must stay in the shadows," Lachlan told her as he pulled the hood of her cloak over her thick, black hair. "Who knows if Dermott is looking for his wife or those who might have helped her."

Deciding his argument was valid, she kept her head down as Lachlan took her hand to lead the way. It somehow felt right and good to have her hand in his. It also made her feel safe. *Lord, what would I have done had he not been here?*

It suddenly dawned on her that she still had no idea why he was here and what he was doing at the Tickled Pickle of all places. Curiosity was getting the better of her.

"Lachlan?" she said as they paused at the end of an alley for Lachlan to scan the street and pathways. "Ye never did tell me why ye are here."

"That is a story best told when we have more time," he said.

Was he being intentionally evasive?

Her mind began to race. Had he come to Inverness to seek the comfort of one of Euphemie's ladies? Just the thought made her angry. To think of him in the arms of any other woman made her blood boil. Wasn't it only a few weeks ago that he had asked for her hand? Was he the kind of man she used to share her time with? The married kind who sought pleasure in another woman's arms?

Nay, she realized as soon as she'd thought it. Lachlan was far too honorable and loyal to do such a thing.

Out of the shadows and onto the street that ran along the river and would eventually lead them to the brothel. All the while, her mind conjured up all sorts of reasons as to why he was here. And not a one of them brought her any peace of mind.

"It was nay to seek the talents of Euphemie or the women who work for her," he told her as the hurried down the street. "I give ye my word I will explain it to ye later."

Just why she felt so relieved she couldn't rightly say. But relieved she was. Oh, she knew she had no right to feel jealous, however knowing that didn't make the feeling any less intense.

"I am glad ye are here," she admitted.

He chanced a sideways glance at her. "I am as well, Keevah. For I have surely missed ye."

"Ye have?"

"I have thought of little else besides ye since the day I left," he said as he gave her hand a gentle squeeze.

Knowing he'd been thinking of her made her heart skip a beat right before dread set in. They couldn't be together, not in the way he wanted. He needed a good woman as his wife. A woman without a past. Still, it did make her heart flutter knowing he *did* want her. Oh, how she hated the contrariness in her heart.

RESTING WAS EASIER SAID THAN DONE. BRIGID HAD BEEN SO relieved to see Keevah return that she refused to let the woman out of her sight for even a moment. She sat on Keevah's lap throughout the meal and insisted on sitting beside her while she napped.

Napping while a five-year-old child is staring at you is rather difficult. Thankfully, after a little bit of coaxing, Brigid lay down beside Keevah and fell fast asleep.

Sleep, however, was not as easy for Keevah. She simply couldn't take her gaze away. For an hour, she studied every inch of the Brigid's sweet face, her curly black locks, her thick dark lashes, cherubic cheeks, and little fingers.

She hadn't been able to that since the day she was born. Five years, three months, two weeks and two days ago. She knew, because she had counted every one of the days since she had placed her daughter into Kiernan's arms.

There was not a day that passed without thinking of her babe. Seldom did she worry over the babe's safety because she knew Kiernan was a good person and would love Brigid as if she had come from her own womb.

It had been difficult giving her daughter away; it had not been a decision made lightly. There were many times she had regretted her decision but whenever the regrets and guilt grew, she reminded herself 'twas out of her love for her daughter that she'd given her away. There was no way she could have raised her on her own, at least not at that point in her life. She was a prostitute. Raising a child within the walls of a brothel was impossible.

Her daughter needed a good home, with parents who loved her, people who could care for her, nurture her and help her grow into a fine woman.

Dermott had fooled her. He had led her to believe that fatherhood had changed him.

How could she have been so wrong?

Brigid sighed sweetly as she slept. Content, Keevah supposed, at least in her sleep.

Love, deep and true, swelled inside her heart, filling her eyes with tears. *Oh, my sweet babe, how I have missed ye.*

Guilt reared its ugly head. Her heart cracked thinking of Kiernan whose cold body now lay somewhere in the Black Friar Priory to be properly laid to rest. Dead because Keevah hadn't kept her safe. Dead because she'd married a most foul, ugly man. Dead because Keevah had ran away.

It should be Kiernan here with Brigid, nae me. I may have given birth to Brigid, but Kiernan is and always will be her mum.

LACHLAN SAT IN A CHAIR BY THE DOOR; HIS LEGS STRETCHED OUT and arms over his chest. He dosed off and on only because he knew Euphemie's man, Charles, had all entrances to the brothel guarded. Both against Dermott as well as the killer at large. He sat, listening at first to Keevah and Brigid whispering, then their steady breaths after falling asleep.

He could not help but wonder what was going through Keevah's mind. How long had it been since she'd seen her friend or her daughter? Had she given any further thought to his proposal?

He'd marry her today if she'd have him. Together, they could raise Brigid to be a fine woman. Together, they could bring the Chisolms around and make the keep and lands even more prosperous, sans the coin earned from the brothel of course.

Before coming above stairs, he had signed the deed to the building and the business over to Euphemie. He could sense she still didn't believe there wasn't a catch, even after signing the document.

In her line of business, 'twas probably prudent to be more a pessimist than your average fellow. They might cater to a higher class of clientele, but it was still a rather shady business.

Tonight, tonight he would have a heartfelt discussion with Keevah. The one he had wished they had been able to have before he left to begin his new life. The one in which he would give her the words of his heart and convince her that marrying him wasn't such a bad idea.

He must have been more tired than he realized and had fallen into a deep sleep. He didn't hear Brigid slip from the bed; didn't even know she was standing right beside him until she tugged on his tunic.

In a soft, sweet whisper she said, "I has to pee and Keevah is asleep."

He rubbed the sleep from his eyes with the backs of his hands, stood, and took the child by the hand. Quietly, they tiptoed from the room and down the stairs in search of Euphemie.

The moment they reached the second-floor landing, he realized, mayhap, he should have awakened Keevah. There were a few men in the drawing room, and each was surrounded by beautiful women. A few of those women were in nothing but their chemises. The others were dressed in fine gowns. Gowns that revealed a little too much of their bosom.

He picked Brigid up and carried her down the stairs hoping to shield her from the goings on. A woman in a plain brown dress was coming out of the kitchen with a heavy tray just as he was trying to enter.

"What do ye need?" she asked, pausing in the little hallway between the two spaces.

"I has to pee," Brigid told her.

The woman rolled her eyes and told them to wait.

She returned with an empty tray and a scowl in short order. "Euphemie said nothin' about child mindin' when I took the position as cook and housekeeper," she said as she glowered at Lachlan.

Her scowl disappeared the moment she took Brigid from his arms. "Ye can call me Auntie Bess, lassie. I will help ye."

Lachlan was much relieved to have the woman's help. He didn't know the first thing about children.

KEEVAH SLEPT LIKE THE DEAD UNTIL LATE IN THE AFTERNOON. When she woke, she found Brigid had at some point slipped from the bed. Panic rose as she sat upright, her sleepy eyes searching the room before she heard a giggle.

There, on the floor near the brazier sat the two people she loved most in life. They were playing with little wooden toys. Brigid was making the little carved horse 'gallop' across the floor. "Then what happened?" she whispered.

"The warrior slayed the infidel, sending him straight to hell," he whispered back.

Appalled, for she didn't believe he should be telling such a story to someone so young, she cleared her throat.

"Ah! Our queen has awakened," Lachlan said, giving her a wink.

Brigid spun around and smiled. "Keevah!" She all but flung herself into Keevah's arms. "Lachlan and I were playin'," she told her. "He just slayed the infidel."

"So I heard," Keevah said, giving Lachlan a glare that said she didn't approve.

Brigid hugged her tightly before returning to her spot on the floor. "Is that when the people were freed?"

"Aye, lass, that is when the people were freed."

She nodded approvingly. "Good." Grabbing up another wooden toy, she asked, without looking, "Have ye ever slayed an infidel?"

He scratched his stubbled jaw and pretended to think about it. "One or two, I suppose."

Worried over where the conversation or story would go next, Keevah left the bed. "Mayhap it is time to eat?"

"Auntie Bess gave us sweet cakes," Brigid told her.

"Auntie Bess?" Keevah asked.

Lachlan was still smiling warmly at the little girl. "The cook. She and Brigid have become fast friends."

"I see. Well, mayhap yer auntie Bess will give us a sweet cake?" She held out her hand to Brigid.

"It is awfully busy below stairs," he said hoping she'd catch on. Getting to his feet he said, "I will go."

"Really, Lachlan," she said. "Do ye nae think I dunnae ken what goes on here?"

He leaned in and whispered, "I ken ye do. But should Brigid?"

She supposed he was right. "Verra well, I shall go below stairs. Ye stay here with Lachlan." Before leaving, she gave him a stern look of warning that said, no more terrifying stories of death or killing infidels.

❦

THE CONVERSATION HE SO DESPERATELY WANTED TO HAVE WITH Keevah hadn't taken place as he'd planned. Murdoch had returned in time for the evening meal, fell onto a pallet and fell asleep almost instantly. But first, Keevah had made him promise to tell her everything that had transpired after she and Lachlan had left that morn.

Keevah washed Brigid's face and hands and combed her hair until it shined. They talked for at least an hour before they too, fell asleep.

In the morning, he told himself. *When this place is quiet.*

While everyone else slept like the dead, Lachlan could not. He had far too much on his mind. Most of his thoughts surrounded Keevah and their future together. He wanted her as his wife, his partner, the mother of his children. He wanted her in every good sense of the word.

As he lay in the dark of night, he imagined their keep filled with children running about, happy, content, and protected. Should anything ever happen to him, he had no doubt that Richard and Aeschene would take care of them.

He imagined Keevah lying in his arms in their own bed, a soft fire crackling in their hearth. Warm, soft furs draped across warm, soft skin. Their nights filled with loving and passion. Their days busy, filled with all the good things life had to offer.

A scraping sound floated up from the alley below, breaking his quiet reverie. Stealthily, he leapt from the cot, silently withdrew his sword as he pulled back the fur.

A dense, heavy fog filled the night sky.

Someone is out there. The hair on the back of his neck stood on end as his pulse quickened. Straining his eyes, he quieted his breathing to listen.

A long, tense moment passed by before he heard another sound. The soft footfalls of boots across cobblestone. Slow, careful, measured steps.

Quickly, he slid his feet into his boots, grabbed his cloak and made his way down the stairs. Ignoring the noisy, boisterous goings on in the bedchambers, and even noisier events taking placing in the greeting room, he went to the kitchens and slipped out the back door.

Standing in the foggy alley, he paused to listen. The sounds of raucous laughter coming from the brothel and the tavern next door were the only sounds he could now hear.

Stealthily, he made his way to the end of the alley, paused and listened, scanning the area all around him.

After a long while, he felt certain whomever had been here was now gone. Just as quietly as he had arrived, he went back inside and slid into his cot.

He didn't sheath his sword, instead, kept it right beside him.

His gut told him the footfalls were a harbinger of things to come.

Chapter Thirteen

If he had ever possessed a doubt about the rightness of his work, it was immediately relinquished the moment he saw Keevah step out of the brothel and into the alleyway.

Oh, he'd been watching, waiting, learning to see how long it took before Forveleth's dead body had been discovered. The faster the body was discovered the more exciting the game was. Tempting fate? He thought not; 'twas all part of the game.

He'd been just another face in the crowd as he'd been the previous times. Just another nosy onlooker. He'd even commented once or twice, clucking his tongue, looking appalled. "What is this world comin' to?" he had pronounced at the discovery of Mary Andrews's body. He'd repeated the same statement again at Forveleth's.

But because he was so average looking and no one of import, no one paid him a bit of attention, which was good. It kept the game going just a bit longer.

Aye, he was doing God's good work, but should a man not take pride in what he did? Or take a moment of enjoyment from it?

Did a carpenter not stand back to look at what he'd created with a good measure of pride? Did the baker not enjoy his task and make a jest or two with his customers? He sincerely believed that a man ought to enjoy the work he did.

And he was going to sincerely, truly enjoy taking Keevah's life from her.

His heart was still happily beating against his chest after killing Forveleth. Oh, he could go days or weeks even, drunk on the heady scent of fresh blood, reliving the moment over and over again. Satisfied for days, if not weeks.

Keevah, he decided, was heaven sent. If God didn't want her dead, then he wouldn't have put her in his path.

Not once in all these months had he veered from his plans. Each kill was methodically planned, gone over in his mind repeatedly, planning for every contingency. He took great pride in his work, after all.

Just as a carpenter makes painstaking plans to build a cabinet or trunk or chair, he made painstaking plans for each kill. Sometimes he would plan two at a time, always one step ahead. Three of his kills had taken weeks to plan, but only moments to enact.

But Keevah? Something told him he'd have to plan a bit more quickly. With the experience of the seven kills, he felt confident that just this once, he could work more quickly to set his plan in motion.

But the killing? He would take his sweet time with the killing.

Aye, he was going to thoroughly enjoy killing her.

Chapter Fourteen

K eevah woke before dawn and for the first time in an age, she actually felt well rested. Feeling far too warm and content, she lay in the early morning hours, watching her daughter sleep next to her. Lachlan was just across the way, on his back, with one leg drawn up. Even in his sleep, he was a handsome man.

His blond hair was pulled away from his face, gathered into a bit of leather, the rest falling across his shoulders. A longing, deep and intense, tugged at her heart. He was the man she would give anything to spend the rest of her life with. The man she wanted to have children with.

If he had shown her anything in the past two days it was his unyielding sense of duty. He'd also proven time and again, that her past -which was now thoroughly entwined with her present - truly didn't matter to him. If he didn't love her, he would have left by now.

And the way he was with Brigid? Playful, adoring, almost doting. Like a good father should be.

She knew he knew the truth about Brigid. She had seen it in his eyes the first time he saw her. As yet, he hadn't mentioned it and she wasn't sure if that was a good thing or not. Mulling it over for some time, she decided 'twas just Lachlan being honorable. Besides, they truly hadn't had a moment alone in order to have that discussion.

Still, she worried, deep down, he might not be able to forgive her for giving away her child. For now, he was keeping them safe until they had properly buried Kiernan. Once that task was done, he would see her safely back to the MacCullough keep.

Then he would leave.

He would go on with his life and she with hers.

'Twas too painful to think about. She'd been given a taste of what her life would be like without him in the weeks they'd been separated. And now, God was giving her a glimpse at what could be, merely to punish and torment her for her sins. Mayhap, had she not chosen the life of prostitution ...

She had to force herself to push all those 'what ifs' aside. 'Twas simply unbearable. Instead, she had to focus on what was to be. She would take Brigid back to her home with the MacCulloughs and raise her as her own. And if anyone were to question why the child resembled her so closely, she would simply tell them one little lie; she is my niece, my sister's babe. 'Twas only a half-truth. Aye, lying was a sin. She'd simply add that to the long list of other sins she'd committed in her seven and twenty years on God's earth. What was one more sin among the many?

Brigid snuggled in closer, burrowing under the heavy blanket. Lord, how grateful she was the child felt safe with her. Last night, during the evening meal, she had broken down into tears, missing her mum. 'Twas gut wrenching to see the child so upset. All she or Lachlan could do was hug her and offer words of comfort.

Sharing a few stories from their childhood together seemed to lift Brigid's spirits. She actually managed to giggle when Keevah had told her about the time she and her mum got their bottoms paddled for sneaking into the Burly Bear tavern when they should have been sleeping.

That was a lifetime ago. Oh, how she wished she could go back to those carefree days. To see her parents dance in the candlelight, so much in love with one another. To see her brothers running and playing together.

She had to push those thoughts aside as well. Thinking about the past was just as painful as thinking about the future.

Floating in from the alley below were the sounds of the city coming awake. She could hear women talking as they tended to their morning chores. This in turn made her think of Forveleth and all the others, sending shivers of dread racing up and down her spine.

Lord, I pray there are nae more women killed by this madman! I dunnae care if ye strike him dead or if ye help Ewan to catch him. But please, make him stop.

BRIGID WAS OF THE BELIEF THAT IF SHE WERE AWAKE, THEN everyone else should be as well. She smiled sleepily at Keevah and declared the need to relieve her bladder.

After helping the child tend to her morning ablutions, Brigid crawled on top of Lachlan. He feigned sleep.

"'Tis time to wake, Laird Lachlan," she said.

He snored loudly which made her giggle. "I want to play," she told him.

He snored again.

Brigid looked to Keevah for help. "He will nae wake up."

"Mayhap ye should try ticklin' him?" Keevah said as she began to tickle Lachlan's ribs. He retaliated by growling playfully as he tickled Brigid. She giggled and said, "I did nae tickle ye! She did!"

A moment later, he grabbed Keevah and pulled her into the bed. Giving her a bit of her own medicine, he tickled her ribs until she begged him to stop.

Murdoch woke during the melee. With a heavy sigh, he said, "Some of us are tryin' to sleep."

They ignored him and continued their horseplay.

Gruffly, he got to his feet and quit the room, cursing under his breath.

It hit Lachlan then, like a bolt of lightning. *This. This is what I want our lives to be.* The sheer joy in Keevah's eyes tugged at his heart. Laughing, playing with her daughter. This is the life she should have had all along.

Without much thought, he pulled her to his chest and held tight.

When she saw the look in his eyes, her smile faded, turning to a blend of fear and confusion. "What is wrong?" she asked.

"I want to kiss ye," he said, his voice not but a low whisper. "If ye will allow it."

LATER, YEARS LATER, SHE MIGHT ADMIT THE TRUTH OF THE MATTER. But for now, she tried to convince herself 'twas naught more than curiosity that made her nod her head.

His lips, hot, soft, touched hers. Tenderly, oh so very tenderly. The entire world faded away and there was no one but the two of them.

She'd been kissed many times, by many different men.

But this?

Nay, this was not like any other. Soft, warm, sweet, and tender. Just a hint of what could be if she were to ever let her guard down or let her heart feel exactly what it wanted to.

All at once she felt blissfully happy, content, safe, curious, excited.

Then he stopped. Pulled away. Just. Like. That.

She did the unexpected then and kissed *him*. Just as sweetly as he'd kissed her. And all those wonderful feelings came rushing in again.

'Twas Brigid's innocent giggle that brought her back to the here and now. "Are ye two gettin' in love?" She scrunched her shoulders and continued to giggle.

Neither one of them were brave enough to answer the question. Oh, they knew the answer. But fear kept them from voicing it.

LONG AFTER THE NOONING MEAL, WHILE BRIGID NAPPED peacefully on the cot, Lachlan and Keevah sat near the brazier. For a long while, neither of them said a word. The kiss had affected each of them in ways neither could have foreseen.

Wanting very much not to broach the subject that hung in the air like smoke from a blazing fire, she decided to talk about the murdered women. 'Twas a far easier topic than the kiss or how it might or might not affect their future.

"Have ye heard from Ewan or Murdoch?" She tried to sound indifferent, but knew she'd failed miserably.

"Nay," he said with a shake of his head. He was staring at the fire, lost, she surmised from his blank expression and focused gaze, in his own thoughts.

"I have been thinkin'," she said, scooting her chair a bit closer to his so that she might speak more softly. "Why?"

"Why what?" he asked, his gaze still focused on the flames.

"Why do ye suppose he does it?"

He turned to look at her, his brow knotted in confusion. "What does it matter?"

"Ye see, I was thinkin' if we could figure out the 'why' we might be able to figure out the 'who'." She thought it a most excellent concept. Lachlan, however, seemed perplexed.

"He kills because he is insane."

As if that explained everything. Rolling her eyes, she scooted even closer. "Men kill for all sorts of reasons, Lachlan. They kill for gold, or they kill in battle. Some might kill out of jealousy or vengeance. Aye?"

"Aye," he said, drawing the word out as if he were trying to catch up to her way of thinking.

"But this man? He kills *former* prostitutes. Women with at least one child. Why them? If 'tis the prostitutes he hates, why nae kill those who are actually prostitutes? Why kill only women who used to be?"

He gave it a good deal of thought. In the end, he had no earthly idea and admitted such.

"It does nae make any sense," she told him.

"I agree, it does nae. Mayhap if Ewan ever catches him, he can ask him."

Her eyes grew wide with excitement. "Och! I would love to hear that conversation!"

"Are ye daft?" he exclaimed, his voice louder than he wanted.

They both looked to see if they'd awakened Brigid. Seeing she was still fast asleep, Keevah answered his question. "Nay, but I am curious. I cannae explain why, but I am."

He scratched the back of his neck as he shook his head. "I am nae curious as to the why," he told her. "But I would sure as hell like to know who. I pray Ewan is able to stop this fiend before he kills again."

"And why only in the morning?" she wondered aloud. "And where does he kill them? It cannae be far. All of the bodies have been found verra close together. How far could he go, carryin' a dead woman, without bein' noticed?"

While he could agree she was asking some very intelligent questions, he found the entire topic macabre. "Keevah, we need to away this place." He didn't wait for her to protest. "Neither of us can afford to wait until spring. What if Dermott comes lookin' for Brigid?"

She hated the fact that he was right. The longer they stayed, the greater the risk of Dermott either seeing them or discovering where they were. "Can ye give me one more day?" she asked.

"Aye," he said, unable to deny such a simple request. "And I will also give ye a promise."

She tilted her head to one side, most curious.

"If we cannae bury yer friend on the morrow, I promise to bring ye back in the spring."

Tears pooled in her eyes. "But I fear she cannae wait that long," she told him. The thought of her friend not being properly buried made her want to weep.

"The friars will take care of her," he told her, placing a heavy arm around her shoulders. "Ewan gave me his word."

Swiping away her tears, she finally acquiesced. "I ken ye are right, Lachlan. But I find nae comfort in it."

"I ken, lass. I ken."

Chapter Fifteen

Keevah decided to take advantage of the quiet and left Lachlan with Brigid to go below stairs. She needed time to think, to parse out everything taking place in her life right now.

On the landing, she met a young woman coming out of one of the bedchambers. Keevah didn't recognize her. But then, many of the people she knew from her time here had moved on or left the business entirely.

She was a very pretty lass, with long blonde hair and bright blue eyes. She wore a dark purple gown, the hem and sleeves trimmed in gold, Although Keevah didn't know her, she apparently knew about Keevah. "I am terribly sorry to hear about yer friend," she said sincerely.

Keevah thanked her.

"I am Clarice," she said. "Euphemie speaks very highly of ye."

"She is a good woman," Keevah said with a fond smile. She took note then of the satchel in one hand and her cloak draped over the other. "Are ye goin' somewhere?"

"I am," she said. "I cannae wait to be gone from here." She shivered as if she were repulsed.

"I dunnae understand," Keevah said. The Tickled Pickle was the finest establishment in all of Inverness.

With wide eyes, Clarice said, "Have ye nae heard about the Slasher?"

So they have given him a name. "Is that what they are callin' him?"

Nodding, she answered in the affirmative. "I want as far away from here as I can get. 'Tis too terrifyin' now to even step foot out of doors in broad daylight, let alone after dark."

She couldn't blame her for her concern. "Did ye ken any of the women who were killed?"

"I knew two of them," she said as she glanced over the railing to the greeting room below.

The woman was clearly nervous, and who could blame her.

"Where will ye go?"

"Edinburgh," she replied. "I have family there."

"How will ye get there?"

Nervously, Clarice shifted the satchel from one hand to the other. "I have a friend who is takin' me. He should be here soon."

The sound of a door closing below stairs startled the poor young woman. She jumped, clutching her satchel to her chest, her eyes darting here and there.

"Mayhap ye would like a bit of warm cider while ye wait for yer friend," Keevah suggested.

"Or mayhap a large dram of whisky," she said, holding her hand to her chest.

Keevah smiled warmly. "I think we can arrange that."

***

KEEVAH AND CLARICE SAT IN THE QUIET KITCHEN. KEEVAH HAD A large mug of warm cider while Clarice sipped on whisky.

"I am certain the madman will be caught soon," Keevah said, doing her best to be positive and encouraging.

Clarice shook her head. "They will never catch him. He is too smart."

"What makes ye say that?" Keevah asked.

"He has killed more than a dozen women," she told her.

Believing 'twas exaggerated rumors the woman spoke of, Keevah corrected her. "There have only been seven."

"Nay," Clarice argued. "There were others. The killin' started a year ago. Did ye nay ken that?"

As far as she knew, the killings had begun only a few months ago. "But Ewan said there have only been seven. The killin' started in September. What makes ye think there are more?"

Clarice downed the rest of her whisky and immediately poured another. "Because one of them lived."

Stunned, Keevah leaned over the table, her eyes wide. "Lived?" Ewan never mentioned that.

"Aye, she did." Clarice stared at the mug in her hands as she slowly shook her head back and forth.

"Who is she? How did she survive?"

"Her name is Deirdre MacAllister," she said before taking a long pull of the amber liquid. "She has nae been the same since the attack."

"Ye ken her? Ye have talked to her?"

Nodding her head slowly, she said, "Euphemie, Dora, and I did. Charles was the one to find her. He brought her here."

Keevah's mouth fell open. Why hadn't Euphemie told her this? "What happened?"

Another long pull emptied her cup. She poured herself another. "I do nae like to talk about it."

"Please, I want to help. We need to stop this man from killin' again."

"Like I said, they will never catch him. He is too smart."

Keevah refused to accept it.

Clarice drained the entire contents of her mug and slammed it down on the table. "I must go. He will be here soon." She stood up and grabbed her cloak from the back of the chair. "Ye should leave, Keevah. As soon as ye can. This monster is not done killin'."

"Please, ye must tell me what ye know," Keevah pleaded. If there truly was a survivor then she might be able to tell them important details that would lead to the man's capture.

"Talk to Euphemie," Clarice said as she picked her satchel up from the floor. "Talk to Euphemie."

THE MUFFLED SOUND OF WINTER MADE THE SILENCE KEEVAH FOUND in the greeting room even eerier. The space was empty, which was odd for this time of day.

A low burning fire crackled in the hearth. Candles flickered ever so gently. Keevah shivered and drew her shawl more tightly around her shoulders. No one was about, save for Euphemie and Charles. They were speaking in hushed tones near the entry doors.

Keevah couldn't hear what they were saying but it must have been rather serious. Charles's face was unreadable, as always. But Euphemie? She looked bloody angry.

When their conversation ended, Charles nodded before he left the room and headed down the hallway. Euphemie saw Keevah and her expression changed. Her smile, however, didn't quite reach her eyes.

"I need to talk to ye," Keevah said.

"I dunnae have time right now," Euphemie said as she started across the room.

"Please, Euphemie, 'tis important."

Frustrated, she stopped abruptly. "We have just been ordered to close our doors until further notice," she said gruffly. "Is it as important as that?"

Confusion blended with concern. "Who? Who ordered ye closed?"

Her expression said she thought Keevah as intelligent as a mouse. "The sheriff. Who else?"

"But why?"

"He says it is to keep the women safe. But I dunnae believe him. He has been tryin' to shut us down forever. The bloody, self-righteous bastard."

"Safe? Safe from what?"

With a roll of her eyes and a shake of her head she said, "Who do ye think?"

Keevah instantly felt foolish for asking the question. "That is what I want to talk to ye about. The madman."

"Dunnae ye mean the Inverness Slasher?"

"Whatever ye choose to call him," Keevah said.

Euphemie shook her head dismissively. "I dunnae have time to share stories and rumors. I must figure out a way to keep my doors open. The ladies are depending on me."

"Then help the sheriff catch him."

Euphemie laughed sarcastically. "Have ye gone mad? First of all, the sheriff does nae truly care about dead whores. He only cares about shuttin' me down. And how on earth can I help him catch this murderer?" Truly, she was beyond exasperated.

"By telling me about the survivor."

KEEVAH SAW IT, JUST A FLASH OF SOMETHING SHE COULDN'T QUITE name burning in Euphemie's eyes. "I dunnae ken what ye're talkin' about."

"I believe ye do," Keevah replied. She was trying to keep her tone even. She admired Euphemie for so many reasons and owed her a lifetime of gratitude and, above all else, her respect.

Pursing her lips together, the other woman remained quiet, refusing to discuss the matter.

"Euphemie, ye and I have known each other for many years. I owe my life to ye. I owe ye a tremendous debt for what ye did for me, for Kiernan, and Brigid. I want only to help."

"Help?" she scoffed.

"Aye, help."

Euphemie let loose a heavy sigh. "Honestly, I dunnae ken what ye hope to accomplish or how ye think ye can help."

Keevah took a seat by the fire. "I believe the more information we have on this madman, the better our chances of capturing him."

She laughed then, sarcastically. "Ye have lost yer mind, lass."

"Have I?" she challenged. She waited, pleading with her eyes.

Euphemie threw up her hands in defeat. "Verra well," she said as she sat on the chaise. "But I dunnae believe anything I have to say will help."

"It might not help," Keevah admitted. "But 'tis worth a try."

"'Twas about six months ago," Euphemie began. "Ewan thinks the killins dinnae start until September, but I tell ye he is wrong."

Keevah remained quiet on that matter and listened intently to the story unfold.

"'Twas the first part of April, a pretty spring morn. They found the first girl, face down in the river. She'd had her throat slashed. The sheriff did nae even come to see. He sent the grave diggers." Staring at the fire she shook her head as if she still couldn't believe his disregard for any of the victims.

"A few weeks later, another woman was found. Her throat slashed and tossed into the river. Six women; good, kind women. All dead. Their throats had been slashed and their bodies tossed into the river like garbage. And still, the sheriff did nothin'."

Tears began to form, but she kept them at bay. "'Twas August, I think, that Ewan was sent to work for the sheriff, as a deputy."

"Sent?" Keevah asked, her curiosity piqued. "By whom?"

"I dunnae ken," Euphemie replied in a low voice. "I think by then word had begun to spread about all these dead women. Mayhap the king?"

'Twas possible. Keevah made a mental note to ask Ewan the next time she saw him.

"'Twas in September that he stopped tossin' them into the river. He started leavin' them around town, as if he were showin' the world what he could do."

Why did Ewan believe there were only seven victims? Did he not know about those in the river?

"'Twas late October when he took Deirdre MacAllister," she paused and took in a deep, steadying breath. "But she survived."

"How?" Keevah asked breathlessly.

"God's grace?" Euphemie asked with a shrug. "Honestly, I dunnae ken."

"How do ye ken about this woman?"

"She had been left for dead in the alley across the way," Euphemie said. "'Twas Charles who found her. He brought her here straight away."

Charles was a new addition to Euphemie's place. Prior to him, a man named Connor MacDrew was her protector. Connor, she had learned from Bessie earlier, had moved on for reasons no one knew. Keevah was thankful that Charles had come to the woman's rescue.

"I fear I dunnae ken Deirdre," Keevah said. But then she didn't know every prostitute in Inverness either.

Euphemie smiled wanly. "She and I go back many years," she said. "Her mother and mine were good friends." She pulled her gaze from the fire and looked at Keevah. "She had been raped, repeatedly."

Keevah's stomach tightened. "Did she say if she recognized the man who attacked her?"

"Nay," she said with a shake of her head. "She hasn't spoken a word since the attack."

That bit of news was disheartening. Crestfallen, she said, "Nae a word?"

"She could nae speak, Keevah. Her throat had been slashed. 'Twas nae a deep cut, but 'twas deep enough."

Keevah decided to share with her what she had been able to glean from Ewan. "Ewan believes he is takin' them somewhere before he kills them. Somewhere close by."

"Why does he think that?"

"Because there has been very little blood where the women were found. If their throats had been cut where they were discovered, there would be pools of blood."

"I did nae ken that," Euphemie said.

"Did Charles say if 'twas a very bloody scene? Where he found Deirdre?"

"Nay, but we can ask him when he returns."

"Where has he gone?"

"To get reinforcements. He fears he cannae keep my girls safe anymore."

She felt relieved knowing there would be more men here to help protect the women. "Somethin' else we have discovered is that all of these women are former prostitutes."

Euphemie thought on it for a long moment, her brow furrowed in concentration. "Now that ye mention it, I do believe ye are right. None of the women who were killed still worked. Many had moved on, either for marriage or to start legitimate businesses of their own."

"I find that as odd as I do interesting," Keevah admitted. "The men believe this man is someone who hates prostitutes."

Euphemie raised a brow. "Well, that is obvious."

"But if he hates prostitutes, why is he nae killin' those who are still workin'?" That was a question she'd asked repeatedly over the past two days. Thus far, no one had an answer.

"Why do men kill?" Euphemie asked.

Keevah listed the reasons she had given the men the day before. "Coin, jealousy, for God and country."

"Dunnae forget revenge," Euphemie said. "Mayhap this man seeks retribution for some wrong done to him."

That was a very strong possibility. "No matter his reasons, we must find a way to stop him."

"How?" Euphemie asked.

"By speakin' to the one woman who survived."

"THAT POOR WOMAN HAS NAE UTTERED A WORD SINCE THE ATTACK," Euphemie reminded her. "I tell ye she is nae in her right mind."

Keevah supposed she was right. But she couldn't help but to think Deirdre was the key to solving this mystery. "What do ye remember?"

Euphemie's brow furrowed with concentration. "'Twas verra early morn, just like the others. Just before dawn. Charles came runnin' inside yellin' for help. He had Deirdre in his arms. She was bleedin'." Her fingertips went to her throat. "And she was cryin'."

"So she was awake?"

"Just barely. She was delirious. Kept sayin' 'He is goin' to kill. He is goin' to kill us all.'"

A shiver of repulsion traced down Keevah's spine.

"We took her above stairs and sent for a healer. Deirdre floated between cryin' and sleepin' for hours. She was talkin' in her sleep, but it made no sense. The healer did her best. Stitched her up, gave her sleeping potions, bandaged her. There was verra little else to be done."

Keevah's heart broke for Deirdre as she listened to Euphemie tell her story.

"She was like that for days. We truly thought she would die. When she finally woke, all she could do was stare at nothing. She did nae speak a word."

Swiping away a tear, Keevah asked, "Where is she now?"

"Somewhere in the Highlands, with her family. Near the coast I believe. Charles would ken better than I. He escorted her home himself."

KEEVAH MAY NOT HAVE FOUND THE ANSWERS SHE SOUGHT, BUT SHE did feel she knew more about the attacker than before. He had gone from leaving bodies in the river, to leaving them in the alleys. She couldn't help to feel the killer was trying to send some sort of message. But for the life of her she couldn't figure out what that message was.

"Thank ye, Euphemie. For all ye have done for all of us over the years."

The two women were just breaking their embrace when Lachlan and Brigid appeared. He looked relieved to see Keevah. Brigid ran to Keevah and jumped into her arms. "I am awake now," she said as she wrapped her arms around Keevah's neck.

"I can see," Keevah giggled. "Did ye have a good nap?"

Brigid's head bobbed up and down. "I am hungry."

"Well, let us see what Bessie might have for us to eat," Keevah said.

Chapter Sixteen

'T was long after the midnight hour when they were awakened
by the sounds of Brigid screaming. Caught in some hellish
nightmare, she cried out for her mother. "Nay! Nay!" she
screamed, thrashing about the bed.

Keevah sat up and pulled her into her arms. "Wheest, lass, 'tis
naught but a bad dream."

"Dunnae hurt her!" she cried. "Stop!"

Lachlan lit a candle and came to sit by the bed. He rubbed Brigid's
back and did his best to comfort her. Keevah was heartsick. "I want
my mamma," Brigid cried.

The child might as well have ripped Keevah's heart from her chest
for the effect was just the same. Gently, she laid Brigid's head against
her shoulder and tried to soothe her.

"Wheest, lass, wheest," Keevah whispered against the top of her
head. "Everythin' will be alright. Ye will see."

"But I want my mamma," she continued to cry.

"I ken ye do, lass. I miss her too."

Brigid lifted her head and looked at Keevah. She was awake now, or
at least partly so. "Ye do?"

"Aye," Keevah replied with a warm smile and tear-filled eyes. "I truly do. She was a beautiful woman and a verra good mum to ye. She will be missed by many."

"Da will nae miss her," she said. "Da hated her."

Were Brigid an adult, Keevah would have much to say on that subject. For the life of her, she didn't know how to respond.

"My da killed her. She was tryin' to protect me," she said between sobs. "But she would nae let him hurt me."

Fury and hatred for Dermott McInnes blended until her stomach churned. What on earth could this sweet child or her mother have done for him to justify hurting either of them?

"Mr. MacElany would nae let him hurt me either," she said.

"Who is Mr. MacElany?"

"Our neighbors. He heard da yellin' and the table break. He was verra mad with da."

Truly, Keevah didn't wish to hear any more, but knew Brigid was in dire need of talking about that night. "I am verra glad Mr. MacElany came to help ye."

Brigid nodded her head so rapidly her black curls bobbed. "He was verra angry with da."

Who wouldn't have been?

Leaning in, Brigid began to whisper. "I have a secret that I am nae supposed to tell."

Intrigued but not ready to push the matter, Keevah simply sat and listened.

"I am nae supposed to tell," Brigid reiterated. "But I want to tell ye so ye will nae worry about me da."

Worry over her father? Highly unlikely. As far as she was concerned the man could rot in hell for eternity. He'd find no sympathy from her quarter.

"I am sure yer da will be fine." She almost choked on those words.

Brigid shook her head and whispered, "Nay. Do ye want to ken why?"

Keevah nodded.

"Because he is burnin' in hell."

Neither Lachlan nor Keevah could have been more stunned. They shared a quick, confused glance with one another.

"What do ye mean, child?" Keevah asked.

"I am nae supposed to tell," she said. "But Mr. MacElany stopped da from hurtin' us. He put his dirk in da's black heart. That is what Mr. MacElany said." Affecting her most serious and grown-up voice, she mimicked what she had heard. "Ye have a black heart, Dermott and I am sendin' ye to hell."

Keevah tried to brush this information off as the overactive imagination of a little girl. "I am sure ye must have misunderstood."

"Nay," she replied. "I saw him put his dirk into me da's heart. Right here." She pointed to her own chest. "But I dinnae cry."

Keevah was perplexed to say the least.

"I dinnae cry because I was glad Da was dead. He was a mean man. I am nae worried he will take me away because he is dead. But he dinnae get to go to Heaven like my mum did. Because he has a black heart and Mr. MacElany sent him to hell."

Lachlan knelt beside them. "Brigid, I am glad ye told us yer secret." He smiled warmly at her. "But ye must nae tell anyone else. Can ye give me yer word?"

She agreed with a nod. "Because I dunnae want Mr. MacElany to get into trouble."

"That is right, lass. We dunnae want Mr. MacElany to get into trouble." He patted her head before turning his attention to Keevah. "I think we should try to sleep now," he said.

Keevah wasn't sure if she'd be able to sleep or not but decided she should at least make the effort. They had one day left in Inverness. If they couldn't bury Kiernan on the morrow, she would be forced to leave without her.

Lachlan extinguished the candle and crawled back into his own cot. Keevah lay in the dark, one palm on Brigid's chest. While she waited for her to fall asleep, she couldn't help but think of what Brigid had told her.

She didn't know who Mr. MacElany was but she felt she owed him a debt of gratitude.

THEY'D BEEN TUCKED AWAY IN THE ATTIC FOR WHAT WAS BEGINNING to feel like an eternity. It felt as though the walls were to close in on the four of them. Murdoch was just itching to take to the streets looking for any kind of information or tiniest bit of evidence that might lead them to the identity of the killer. This was their last day in Inverness and he didn't like the idea of leaving until they caught the killer.

Lachlan was itching to return to his new keep, find a priest, marry Keevah and get to beginning their lives together. There wasn't a doubt in his mind that she loved him. The one kiss they had shared that afternoon said everything. She loved him.

And what more did a man need other than the love of a good woman? For the life of him, he couldn't think of anything.

Keevah was still consumed with guilt. She'd deserted her friend years ago when she left Inverness the first time. Unable to bury her now, she couldn't help but feel she was deserting her all over again.

Brigid was begging to go out of doors to play. "But why?" she had asked for what seemed the hundredth time. "'Tis nae rainin'."

As if a bit of rain could keep any child from the out of doors. "Mum used to take me out to the garden every day," she told Keevah. "Even when it snowed."

How on earth could they explain to her that there was a raving lunatic on the loose? "I promise ye, as soon as we get to yer new home, ye can play out of doors every day. Even when it snows."

"When?" she asked with a pout. "When will we get to our new home?"

This stubbornness was definitely something she inherited from her birth mother. Kiernan was always the quiet, well-behaved child who was a stickler for following the rules. On those rare occasions when Kiernan did get into trouble, one could guarantee 'twas because Keevah had instigated something.

Lachlan was doing his best not to laugh. Keevah certainly found no humor in it.

"Brigid, we will leave on the morrow. We will be out of doors for at least two days, on horseback. There will be plenty of time for ye then to play." She was doing her best to maintain her temper, but Lord above, this child would try the patience of a saint.

Lachlan was able to divert her attention away from the argument at hand by offering to give her a piggyback ride around the room. She squealed with delight as he sat on the edge of the cot and told her to climb up.

The room was barely big enough to sleep in let alone rough housing. But if it kept Brigid from complaining, Keevah wouldn't argue against it.

After a half an hour of traipsing about the room like a loon, Lachlan began to grow weary. "All right lass, we need to rest."

"But I am nae tired," she told him.

"But I am," he said.

On and on it went the remainder of the evening. Two adults trying to keep one very bored child entertained. They told her stories, sat on the floor and played with the wooden toys, and told more stories. By the time the evenin' meal rolled around, they were both exhausted.

It didn't take long for Brigid to catch on to the fact that if she said she had to pee, one of the adults would take her below stairs. After the fourth such trip, the adults caught on.

They dined on roasted chicken, vegetables, dried fruits, and sweet cakes. With a full stomach, one would hope the child would grow tired, as the adults had. Not Brigid. If anything, she seemed to be energized by the feast.

By the end of the day, Lachlan felt as though he'd been at war for a fortnight. Keevah felt no better. Brigid was excited to bathe in the room off the kitchens. A huge wooden tub that could easily hold two adults was like bathing in the ocean to a five-year-old. Keevah even added some of the scented oils to the warm water.

'Twas Lachlan who carried her above stairs, wrapped in a large, thick drying cloth. All the while Brigid chattered on about the big tub. "Does my hair smell pretty?" she asked. They both leaned in at the same time; Brigid toward his nose, he toward her hair. They met somewhere in the middle with a thunk of their noggins. 'Twasn't the worst pain of his life, but 'twas painful nonetheless. His eyes watered as he cursed under his breath.

"Well?" she asked. "Does it smell good?"

"Aye, lass," he replied as he placed her upon the bed and rubbed his tender nose.

Keevah bit her lip to keep from laughing.

They sat by the brazier, mother and daughter. Keevah helped the child into her chemise and wrapped her in a heavy wool blanket. She made a mental note they would need more clothing for the little girl as one dress and chemise wouldn't do for much longer.

After toweling off Brigid's hair, Keevah combed the curly locks, careful not to cause her any pain or distress when she came across a tangled knot. Brigid began to grow tired as well as quiet.

Warm from her bath, wrapped in the heavy blanket, and the warmth from the fire soon began to make the little girl yawn. Before long, she was nodding off but continued to fight sleep.

When her hair was sufficiently dry, Keevah picked her up and tucked her into the bed. "Are ye nae goin' to sleep with me?" Brigid asked with a yawn.

"I will lass, but first, I must wash yer dress. I will nae be long, I promise. Lachlan is here. Ye will nae be alone for even a moment."

Thankful and relieved she didn't argue or put up a fuss, Keevah kissed the tip of her nose and drew the furs up around her neck. The child was asleep before Keevah even stepped away.

When she turned around, Lachlan was also fast asleep. She resisted the urge to giggle at the sight of him; one leg dangling off the cot and surrounded by Brigid's wooden toys.

Carefully, she picked up the toys and stacked them on the table. She then pulled the dangling leg onto the cot and drew the covers up to his chin. With a contented sigh, she stood up and stretched.

"Are ye nae goin' to kiss my nose?" he asked sleepily.

"Nae, I am goin' to go below stairs to wash out Brigid's dress. 'Tis the only one she has."

He yawned, his eyes still closed, and said, "We shall get her more on the morrow."

He said nothing else and soon, his breaths were deep and steady.

Draping Brigid's dress over one arm, Keevah quietly slipped out of the room.

⁘

Aye, God had certainly blessed him this night!

He had been standing in the dark alleyway, watching the shadows dance across the window in the attic. Keevah was there, he knew it; he could sense her presence. 'Twas as if the air surrounding him vibrated with anticipation, excitement.

Just as he was about to end his reconnaissance, he saw the door open. Light spilled out into the alleyway and a moment later, she walked out.

It all happened so quickly and praise God, he wasn't seen.

She was hanging something up on the line when he approached her, his knife in one hand, his bindings in the other.

"Remember me, lass?" he whispered as he held the dirk to her long neck.

She took in a deep breath, fully prepared to call for help. He didn't give her the chance.

One forceful blow to the back of her head and she collapsed in his arms.

Aye, God was certainly looking out for him this night.

⁘

Keevah tried to open her eyes but the effort was futile. Her skull pounded mercilessly just at the base of her neck. Throbbing, aching, intense. When she tried to lift her arm to rub the ache away, she found 'twas impossible. Why did her head hurt so badly and why couldn't she move her arms.

Her mouth was as dry as wool and she felt cold, very cold. I must be ill, she thought to herself. Even thinking hurt.

"Lachlan," she tried calling out his name but her mouth and throat were far too dry. Dry, scratching, her words were nothing more than a harsh whisper.

Fear crept into her heart. *Brigid. Where is Brigid.*

She struggled to free her thoughts, to make her way through the cobwebs that clouded her mind. 'Twas too much effort to make sense of anything.

Sleep. I need only to sleep for a bit. I will feel better when I wake.

⁂

JUST WHY HE WOKE, HE WAS UNCERTAIN. BUT SOMETHING FELT OFF. Lachlan sat up in his cot and looked around the room. The candle had burned low, the wick nearly burned entirely away.

When he looked at the cot Keevah shared with Brigid, only Brigid slumbered there.

Dread, sheer and unadulterated, spread from his gut to his fingertips.

"Keevah?" he whispered her name as he got to his feet.

He was met with deafening silence.

Quickly, he pulled on his boots and shoved his arms into his tunic before grabbing his sword. He all but ran down the stairs.

There were still a few people huddled together in the greeting room. Charles was standing near the entry doors. "Have ye seen Keevah?" he asked as he raced across the floor.

"Nay," Charles said, his brow furrowing. "I thought ye were all above stairs."

"I fell asleep," Lachlan said. "She left to wash out Brigid's dress. That was at least an hour ago."

Worry settled in Charle's intense eyes. "Has anyone here seen Keevah?" he asked as he crossed the floor. Lachlan was right behind him.

"We have nay seen her," one of the women said, looking quite concerned.

Charles led the way into the kitchens, searching, while Lachlan called out her name. Bessie appeared from the larder, confusion etched in her brow.

"Have ye seen Keevah?" Lachlan asked, his tone laced with worry.

"Aye, mayhap and hour ago," she replied. "She was washin' out Brigid's dress."

"Where did she go after?"

"I dunnae ken," Bessie said as she placed a hand on her heart. "I thought she went back above stairs."

"Ye did nae see her leave?" Lachlan all but barked his question.

Bessie shook her head rapidly. "Nay, not since she stepped out to hang Brigid's dress on the line."

FOR A LONG MOMENT, LACHLAN SWORE HIS HEART DID NOT BEAT. But when it began to beat again it pounded ferociously against his chest. Blood rushed in his ears as fury enveloped him.

He flung the door open and stepped out into the darkness. Charles came out, holding a lighted torch. Lachlan had only taken one step when he felt something under his feet.

"What is it?" Charles asked as they crouched down to get a better look.

As soon as the torchlight fell over the object, he knew something terrible had happened to Keevah.

"Brigid's dress," he said as he picked the garment up.

Charles knew as well as Lachlan that something was afoot.

Lachlan swallowed back the bile of fear creeping up from his stomach. "He has taken her."

"Who?" Charles asked.

"The madman."

WHEN NEXT KEEVAH WOKE, HER HEAD DIDN'T HURT NEARLY AS much. There was still an intense throbbing at the base of her skull, but she no longer felt she was just moments from death.

Slowly, she opened her eyes in hopes of getting a grasp on what was happening. She was met with darkness. Her teeth chattered as she tried to determine why she was so profoundly cold.

For a long while, nothing made sense. Her room was cloaked in darkness, she felt as strong as a blade of grass trampled into a pile of mud, and she could not remember ever being this cold.

'Twasn't until she tried to sit that she realized something was wrong. Her hands and feet were bound. She wasn't on her cot as she had assumed. She was strapped to a hard surface.

Terror seized every fiber of her being. She struggled against her bonds as her heart pounded relentlessly against her chest. Blood rushed in her ears as her breaths became ragged with fear.

From somewhere within the cold room, she heard a man's laughter break through the silence. 'Twas hideous.

"Struggle all ye wish, 'twill do ye no good."

Keevah sucked in a deep breath and closed her eyes. God help me.

Chapter Seventeen

There would not be a building, a rock, or a place in Inverness that Lachlan would not tear apart looking for Keevah. No stone would be left unturned.

Murdoch raced to the inn where the rest of their men were staying. They came running, armed to the teeth, angry as hell, and fully prepared to do battle.

They used the Tickled Pickle as a staging location. 'Twas just after midnight on this bleak, cold winter's night. The moon shone brilliantly, which would aid in their search.

Charles had gathered more men to help. Lachlan did not bother asking for names or histories. He simply wanted the manpower.

Ewan came in right behind Charles.

"When was she taken?" Ewan asked as he thundered through the back door.

"Bessie last saw her three hours ago," Lachlan informed him.

Ewan gave a curt nod of his head. "Then there is still time."

"How do ye ken that?" Murdoch asked.

Ewan began to answer when Lachlan flung open the door. "Ye can discuss that while we look," he ground out. "I will nae waste time on yer theories or assumptions."

"Lachlan, we should have a plan," Charles said. "To make certain we do nae search the same places twice.

His fury and anger were not allowing him to think clearly. He was glad, however, that Charles suggested it. 'Twas quickly decided that the men would be broken into teams of two and each were assigned a street. Three men would be sent to search along the river. Lachlan, Murdoch, and Ewan would search together.

Ewan spoke up. "He is probably usin' an abandoned buildin'. I would search those first."

Lachlan could not necessarily disagree with that assumption. It stood to reason that the killer would not want anyone witnessing his comings and goings.

He took one last long look at the men crowded into the kitchen and gave a curt nod before opening the door.

More than two-dozen men spilled into the alley. Torches flickered in the night air, casting shadows across the buildings. These were men on a hunt: the hunt for a killer and an innocent woman.

Ewan and Murdoch walked beside Lachlan. "I have been doin' more research," Ewan began. "I think he keeps then for a day or two before he disposes of them."

Fury coursed through Lachlan's veins, white hot, impenetrable. His only thought, his only mission was to find Keevah.

"What do ye mean, he keeps them?" Murdoch asked as they reached the end of the alley.

Lachlan stopped the procession. "Search every buildin', every inn, tavern, every business. Ye search them with or without the owners' permission. Do nae stop until ye find her."

"And if ye do find her," Charles said, "ye bring her back here at once then send word to Lachlan."

THE MEN AGREED AND SOON BEGAN TO FAN OUT. LACHLAN, Murdoch, and Ewan would search the buildings along Chapel Street. Laughter and light spilled out from the few taverns that were still open at this hour. Lachlan thundered down the street, all the while his heart beat mercilessly against his chest.

Fear. Inescapable fear filled his gut. Fear of what was happening to Keevah at this very moment. Fear that she was already dead.

And rage. Rage that any man would dare harm her, let alone any other woman. But she was not just any other woman. She was his. His heart. His entire existence.

He refused to think about his future without her in it. He would not allow his heart or his mind to think of his world continuing without her in it. He would accept nothing less than finding her alive.

The next emotion to assault his senses was guilt. Absolute, unequivocal guilt. He should have insisted they left days ago; that very night. *What were ye thinkin' keepin' her here?* The answer wasn't hard to find. He was trying to endear himself to her. To make her see he could be agreeable, that he loved her no matter what may come.

Ye were so busy tryin' to impress her that ye could nae truly see what danger she might be in. She was just like the others, ye fool. A former prostitute with a child.

His reverie was broken by the discussion between Murdoch and Ewan. "It has to be close to where the other bodies were discovered," Ewan said.

Lachlan came to an abrupt halt, withdrew his dirk and pinned Ewan against a wall. "Ye will nae ever refer to her as that again," he seethed. "She is nae another body. She is a woman, and she is still alive."

TEARS FELL DOWN HER TEMPLES, POOLING ON THE COLD TABLE. Lachlan and Brigid consumed her thoughts. Without a doubt she knew Lachlan was searching for her. She tried to cling to the hope that he would find her before it was too late.

But if he didn't succeed, she also knew he would take Brigid to raise as his own. He would see to it that she had a good life, an education, and she would never have to sell herself in order to survive.

How could I have been so foolish? She'd been so intent on trying to help catch this madman that she didn't stop to think about the consequences. She was just like all his other victims. How had she not seen it? How had she not realized she could be his next victim?

"Oh, ye will be such fun to play with, Keevah," the haunting voice said through the dark. She heard scratching sounds coming from somewhere nearby. A moment later, a flame from a candle grew before dimming ever so slightly. Still, 'twas not enough light to bring her any comfort.

"Why are ye doin' this?" She didn't know where she got the strength to ask the question.

"'Tis God's work I am doin'," he hissed.

Repulsed by his reasons, she scoffed. "God's work?" She swallowed the fear and bile. "Nay, this is not God's work. Ye do it because ye like it."

She heard his rapid footfalls scraping across a wooden floor. He was upon her then, his dirk pricking the skin along her neck. "My enjoyment is God's reward for doin' His good work."

The sickening sound of his voice made her heart race faster. She could feel sweat breaking across her brow and at the nape of her neck.

"'Tis good to see ye so afraid," he whispered. He traced the tip of the dirk down the front of her gown and back again. "I may just keep ye alive longer than the others."

"Who are ye?" she demanded.

His maniacal laughter echoed off the walls. "I will be the last man ever to touch ye," he said. "I will be the last man ye ever let betwixt yer legs. I will be the last face ye ever see. I will be yer last everything."

SIMILAR TO THE ANCIENT STORIES OF BERSERKERS, LACHLAN tore through one building after another, one room after another. He cared not who he terrified in the process. He cared not what laws he might be breaking. He was going to find Keevah if it was the last thing he ever did.

Their search along Chapel street led them to nothing but surprised and angry individuals whose homes they had invaded.

"She must be nearby," he growled as they stood outside a vacant building.

Ewan agreed. "They must be nearby. There is no way he could carry anyone so far without bein' seen." He was careful not to use the words 'bodies' or 'victims' out of fear of being gutted.

Lachlan stepped into the middle of the road and scrutinized their surroundings. "Are we close to where the other women were found?"

Ewan nodded. "Aye, they were all found along Church and Bridge Streets, within a four-block area."

Lachlan tried to picture the map of the city he had seen in Ewan's room. "I dunnae ken Inverness well enough," he said. "I wish to see that map of yers again, the one in yer room."

"I have one here," Ewan said as he withdrew a scroll from his belt.

Murdoch held one side, while Ewan held the other. It was an exact replica of the map on Ewan's wall. Lachlan studied it closely. "All those red marks? Are those where the women were found?"

"Aye, they are."

"What are the blue marks?" he asked.

"Somethin' else I am workin' on," Ewan said. "There were six or seven women found in the river last year."

Lachlan's brow raised. "More dead women?" He was incredulous.

"Aye," Ewan replied. "But I dunnae believe it is the same man. These women were all found along the riverbank. They were nae posed like the others."

"Are ye tryin' to tell me there are two madmen runnin' the streets of Inverness, killin' women?"

Ewan was nonplussed as he stammered, searching for a reply. "But the others, they were found along the river, badly decomposed. 'Twas hard to say how some of them died."

Lachlan's jaw began to ache. "Mayhap he got tired of waitin' for the bodies to be discovered," he ground out. "I just cannae believe this is the work of two men. Have ye found more women along the river recently?"

Ewan's face fell as it began to dawn on him that his previous assumptions were incorrect. Almost sheepishly, he answered the question. "Nay, those stopped in June."

For all his brilliant deductions, Ewan had to admit he was wrong.

Lachlan shook his head and spun on his heals. "Call every man to search the buildings along the river," he called out over his shoulder.

As fast as his feet would take him, he made his way toward the River Ness.

HIS GAME WAS FEAR, SHE WAS CERTAIN OF IT. THE MADMAN WANTED - nay *needed* - to see the abject terror in her eyes.

Keevah refused to give that to him; she would die first.

Although she was certain Lachlan was searching for her, she knew there was a strong possibility he would not find her in time. If that was the case, she would make what last few moments she had left as painful as possible for her attacker.

"Why do ye nae show yer face?" she asked into the darkness. "Are ye afraid?"

"Ye will see my face soon enough, whore."

She laughed and shook her head. "Call me what ye like," she said. "It matters nae to me."

She was doing her best to sound brave, or at the very least, unafraid.

What is he doin'? Keevah could hear shuffling sounds coming from her left. Or was it her right? She had no idea as the candle was too far away. Just a small glow to her left, towards her feet. Scraping sounds, as if he were arranging something on a table. Lord, how she wished she could see!

Her mind raced for a way out, a way to get free. Or a way to prolong the inevitable until Lachlan found her. *If* he found her. The longer she stayed strapped to the table, the more she began to doubt she'd be found alive.

Nay, she told her frightened heart. *I will fight until the bitter end.*

The bindings were made of heavy leather; unbreakable. If she were to be freed, it would have to be by her captor's hands. Or Lachlan's. And she was growing far too impatient and angry to remained tied to a table waiting for rescue. Or death.

Just as she had done in all the other very difficult times in her life, such as when they lost her father, and years later, her mother, she had to be strong, at that time for her brothers. And after their deaths? She had to be strong for herself.

Brigid.

The poor child had already lost the woman she knew as her mother. The only good thing in her life. Keevah refused to let her lose her replacement.

"I need to empty my bladder," she told him, trying to keep her tone as normal sounding as possible.

"Then empty it."

"And ruin my pretty dress?" She hoped she didn't sound like an idiot. Or afraid. Or insane.

He ignored her request. More shuffling and scraping noises from the table.

"What is yer name?" she asked, doing her best to maintain her feigned nonchalance and strength.

More silence.

"Have ye lived in Inverness long?" She was asking the questions as if she had just been introduced to a fine gentleman. Inside, her stomach was twisted into knots.

"Do ye have family here?"

He growled. "Be quiet."

She refused to obey the order. "'Tis awfully cold here. Could I have my cloak?"

He banged something down on the table.

"I really need to use the chamber pot."

When her request went unheeded, she said, "Are ye afraid I will escape?"

He laughed.

"Are ye afraid a wee thing like me could overpower ye?"

Heavy footfalls echoed off the walls coming towards her. "I fear nothin'. God is with me."

'Twas clearly evident that he was frustrated with her. He began yanking and pulling at the leather bonds and soon, her hands were free. She thanked him warmly, just to irritate him. A few quick tugs and pulls and her feet were free.

Before she could do anything, he was standing behind her, his hard fingers digging into her arms. He said nothing as he pulled her down from the table. Needles of pain stabbed at her feet as her heart pounded against her breast.

He began to drag her towards the table with the candle. 'Twasn't until she saw the contents of the table that real fear set in. 'Twas filled with countless knives, hammers, wooden clubs, and various other tools that were certainly meant to inflict pain.

Her blood ran cold.

Forcefully, he pushed her into the corner. "Do nae turn around," he barked his order.

Not brave enough just yet, she did as he said. Her breaths were ragged, and her stomach churned with fear and hatred. Moments later, he was thrusting a chamber pot into her hands.

BY THE TIME LACHLAN REACHED THE RIVER, HIS BLOOD WAS BOILING and rushing in his ears. He paused briefly in the middle of the narrow street that ran between the buildings and the river. The only sound he could hear was the pounding of his heart and the heated blood coursing through his veins.

Taking in a deep breath, he closed his eyes for only the briefest moment. Willing his nerves to settle as if he were preparing for battle, knowing he'd need every one of his senses.

Straining his ears, he could hear the river lapping lazily along the slightly frozen banks. A strong breeze rushed in from the west rustling bits of debris along the docks. Other than the sounds of the river, the breeze, and a few night creatures scurrying about, he could hear nothing.

Holding his torch up, he carefully scrutinized the area. An empty street ahead to his left, the river to his right. Crates, barrels, and other cargo were stacked near the docks.

Something, call it instinct or intuition, made the hair on the back of his head stand on end. *She is here.* He could feel it in every fiber of his being.

Silently, he withdrew his sword and pushed his cloak over his shoulders. Cautiously, carefully, he took slow, measured steps down the street. He wasn't about to wait for Murdoch and Ewan or the others.

Keevah's hands shook so hard she dropped the chamber pot. It clanged against the wooden floor and bounced once before hitting the wall.

She expected her captor to admonish her for being loud. Instead, he laughed, that haunting, maniacal laugh. "'Twas a good thing 'twas empty, aye?"

This was nothing but a game to him. A sick, twisted game whereby he instilled fear and terror into his victims.

From somewhere deep inside, her fear and anger blended into strength. She squatted down and picked up the chamber pot. Slowly, she stood and righted her shoulders. "I cannae go with ye lookin' at me."

Much to her relief, he did exactly as she had hoped. He was right behind her, so close that she could feel his hot breath on her neck. "I think I will watch."

Clutching the chamber pot in both hands, she spun around. As hard as she could, she swung it against the side of his face.

He hadn't expected her attack and stumbled sideways.

Keevah dropped the chamber pot and lunged for the table. Panic stricken, she fumbled around until her fingers wrapped around the handle of one of the many knives. She grabbed it, fully prepared to kill him.

Before she could do anything else, he had come up from behind her and shoved her hard against the table. The force of the push caused the knives and tools to jump and scatter.

"Ye bloody whore!" he screamed as he grabbed a fistful of her hair and yanked her backwards.

A guttural scream formed in her throat as she tried to pull away from him. The more she resisted, the more intense the pain. 'Twas next to impossible to think clearly.

He was dragging her backwards, towards the table he'd had her strapped to before. She knew if he got her back to the table, she was as good as dead.

Instead of pulling away, she planted her feet firmly on the floor and lunged backward against his body with all her might. Caught off guard, he slipped and they fell onto the floor.

Keevah rolled sideways, never once letting go of the knife. She picked up her skirts in one hand and tried to find a door. Terrified, she began screaming as loud as she could.

LACHLAN WAS HALFWAY DOWN THE BLOCK WHEN MURDOCH, EWAN, and the other men approached. He raised his torch and signaled for them to be quiet. They paused, withdrew their swords, and approached him as quietly and as quickly as possible. None said a word as they slowly and silently searched their surroundings.

They'd just reached the end of the block when they heard Keevah's blood-curdling screams. All heads spun towards the sound. They were coming from one of the tall buildings in the center of the block.

With his heart racing, Lachlan ran back towards the terrifying screams. He was certain they were coming from the top floor. He tried opening the door but 'twas locked. Raising one heavy booted foot, he kicked at the door once, then again. It crashed open, splinters of wood flying in all directions.

A few feet ahead was a set of wooden stairs. He took the steps two at a time as he called out her name. "Keevah! Keevah!"

When they reached the second floor landing they could hear a loud crash coming from above stairs. As fast as lightning Lachlan's feet barely touched the steps.

They spilled onto the landing and found a door on either side and one straight ahead. Uncertain which door to open, they began crashing through all three.

⁂

THE DOOR! SHE'D FOUND THE DOOR!

Just as she reached out to grab the handle, his arms were around her waist, pulling her back again. "Ye filthy whore!" he seethed. "Ye are a dead woman, Keevah! I am going to slice ye into a thousand bloody pieces!"

She screamed again, louder and louder as he lifted her off the ground. She kicked and kicked until she remembered the knife in her hand. With a panic-stricken heart, she turned the knife over in her palm and thrust it backwards.

He screamed in agony as the knife tore through the flesh of his thigh. Keevah pulled it out and thrust it again and yet again, until his grip loosened. Covered in blood, the knife slipped from her hands.

Once again, they fell to the floor.

Scrambling to her feet, she didn't bother searching for the weapon. She knew she had to get to the door. If she could just get out of the room, she could run for help.

Just as she was racing toward freedom, she heard a loud bang coming from outside. Torchlight spilled into the space as a shadow stood in the doorway.

It all happened so fast it made her head spin.

The door flung open, banging against the wall just as her attacker wrapped a heavy arm around her neck and began pulling her back. This time, he put a dirk against her neck. "Stop!" he yelled at the shadowy figure. "I will slice her throat if ye take another step!"

The next sound she heard made her heart seize with joy and relief. "Ye will be dead before yer bloody body hits the floor."

The sound of Lachlan's voice was all she needed in order to continue to fight. She grabbed his arm with both hands and bit down as hard as she could.

That was all Lachlan needed in order to send the bloody bastard to the bowels of Hell.

As the Inverness Slasher growled with pain, he let Keevah fall to the floor. In two large, furious strides, Lachlan was upon him.

"Dunnae kill him!" Ewan screamed from behind.

Lachlan thought 'twas the most insane and ridiculous thing he'd ever heard. Ignoring the plea, Lachlan thrust his sword deep into the man's gut.

Chapter Eighteen

Keevah didn't remember falling into Lachlan's arms. She didn't remember the long, quiet walk back to the Tickled Pickle or drinking the sleeping draught the healer had given her.

She slept like the dead until the following evening. Lachlan never once left her side. Neither did Brigid.

When she finally woke, every muscle in her body ached. Even opening her eyes was a challenge. Her head swam and the room spun and for the briefest moment she was certain she was back in that cold, dark, musty room.

Closing her eyes, she took in slow breaths. When her nausea subsided, she opened her eyes again. When her vision cleared, she saw Lachlan's beautiful, handsome face. He was leaning over the bed, holding her hand and smoothing loose strands of hair from her forehead. She let out a long, heavy, relieved breath right before tears filled her eyes.

"Wheest, lass," he whispered warmly. "Ye are safe."

"Is he dead?" It hurt to speak, her voice sounded scratchy and hoarse.

Lachlan nodded as he gave her hand a gentle squeeze.

Brigid climbed onto the bed and squeezed in beside her. "Did ye send the bad man to Hell with my da?" she asked in a most serious tone.

Lachlan looked at Keevah, silently asking for permission to answer the child's question. Keevah gave a slow, tired nod.

"The bad man is dead," he told her.

"Good," Brigid replied before asking, "Did ye hit his head like Mr. MacElany hit da?"

"Brigid, let us nae talk about that right now," Lachlan said. "Keevah needs to rest."

Keevah was glad he'd put a stop to the conversation. "Water," she scratched out as she pointed to her throat. Moments later, he was holding her head and putting a cup to her lips. 'Twas truly painful to swallow, but her mouth felt as dry as dust.

She heard Euphemie's voice coming from near the door. "Brigid, lets ye and I go below stairs and see what Bessie is fixin' for our supper?"

Reluctantly, Brigid climbed down from the bed. Lachlan waited until the door clicked behind them before turning his attention back to Keevah.

"I ken ye're in some pain, lass," he said as he took a gentle hold of her hand.

"Aye," she managed to scratch out.

"I also ken it pains ye to speak."

She nodded her affirmation.

"Good," he smiled. "So ye can do naught but listen."

Here it comes, she thought. *He is bloody furious and who can blame him?*

"The gravediggers were here," he told her. "The ground is still frozen. We have two choices, Keevah. We can come back in the spring or we can take Kiernan with us. Either way, we will be leavin' Inverness just as soon as ye are able to ride."

He certainly didn't sound angry. Nay, his voice was filled with nothing but warmth. "But on the morrow, ye and I will stand before a priest and we will be wed."

Her eyes flew open. Had she the strength to, she would have argued against it. But then she looked into those warm brown eyes and saw nothing but love and a good deal of determination.

"As soon as I realized ye'd been taken by that madman—" his voice cracked ever so slightly. "Keevah, my world came undone. I cannae live this life without ye in it. Ye either marry me on the morrow, or I will wade into the River Ness and let my body be washed out to sea."

There was no doubt in her mind that he was serious.

"I love ye, Keevah. With every fiber of my being, with every bit of my soul, I love ye. I want no other."

She tried to speak but he stopped her. "Please, do nae say I need a better woman," he said. "There is nae better, finer woman in all the world than ye."

Again, she tried to speak but he wouldn't allow her to. "I ken yer past is important to ye. Euphemie has helped me to see that. When I say it matters nae to me, what I mean is that no matter what yer past is, I love ye. The woman ye are now."

She couldn't hold onto her tears any longer. They trailed down her cheeks.

"I also ken that Brigid is yers. When ye are stronger, we will talk about that. But for now, please ken my heart. We will raise her together as our own. And if ye and God are willin', we will give her many brothers and sisters. I will nae live the rest of my life without ye or Brigid in it."

She swallowed hard and tried to speak. This time, when he stopped her, she shook her head. "I am tryin' to say aye, if ye'll listen."

It took a moment for the words to sink in. When the realization that she was finally accepting his proposal set in, he smiled so broadly and brightly, 'twas like balm to her spirits.

"Ye will marry me then?" he asked, just to be certain.

"Aye," she smiled up at him. "Aye."

THEY WERE WED THE FOLLOWING MORNING.

Murdoch stood as his best man. The other men stood behind him, but very few of them were paying attention to the ceremony. They were too busy looking at Euphemie's 'ladies': a dozen beautiful women dressed in their finest gowns. Charles, as always, stood as sentry at the entry door.

One of the ladies had loaned Keevah a beautiful, midnight blue gown. Four of them had spent nearly two hours styling her hair. Braided around the top of her scalp, loose tendrils fell down her back. They had affixed tiny, blue and white dried flowers throughout her black locks.

Lachlan had never seen her looking so regal or happy.

Brigid stood next to Keevah, smiling throughout the ceremony. 'Twasn't that she truly cared about the wedding. Nay, she was looking forward to the sweet cakes Bessie had promised her earlier. She was also filled with anticipation of the adventure of traveling across the highlands on horseback to her new home.

"I love ye, Keevah. I promise to love, honor, protect, and cherish ye all the rest of my days," Lachlan promised before the priest.

Brigid tugged on his tunic. "Me too?" she asked. Those crowded around them laughed quietly at her innocent question.

He smiled, patted her head and said, "Aye, lassie. I promise ye as well."

Keevah gave him the words of her own heart. "I love ye, Lachlan MacCullough. With all that I am. I promise to love, honor, protect, and cherish ye all the rest of my days.

The priest said a prayer over them, made the sign of the cross, and then gave Lachlan permission to kiss his bride.

Gently, he lowered his head and pressed his lips to hers. Warm, sweet, and tender. The room erupted into applause, bringing the kiss to a halt.

Lachlan had refused Euphemie's offer to spend their wedding night in her opulently appointed room. Instead, he'd procured a room at the inn down the street.

As soon as they finished the wedding feast Bessie had so thoughtfully prepared, they said their goodbyes, gave their thanks to Euphemie and Charles, and left the Tickled Pickle behind them.

Night had yet to fall when Brigid finally, blessedly fell asleep. Lachlan had carried her to the little cot near the brazier and gently covered her with a warm fur.

The newly formed family had spent the better part of the day tucked away in a quiet room at the inn. Enjoying one another's company, they had played games and told stories; simple things that meant everything to Keevah.

Although she was still in a goodly amount of pain, Keevah's heart was filled near to bursting with all the love she had for Lachlan, as well as her daughter. 'Twas still difficult to speak as her voice was still hoarse from all the screaming she'd done the night she'd been abducted.

Today was far too special to allow the memories of that night to squirm their way inside. Later, mayhap after they arrived at their new home, she would bring up the matter of the Inverness Slasher. For now, she was simply content knowing Lachlan had killed him. The bloody bastard would never be able to harm another woman again.

Lachlan doused all but one candle before climbing into bed with his wife. He had sworn to himself that he would wait until she had regained some of her strength before making love to her.

But as soon as she slipped off her chemise and snuggled in beside him, that promise faded like fog in the afternoon sun.

They made slow, tender love to each other, intently, methodically exploring each other's bodies. Tender, amorous kisses, soft gentle caresses that neither of them wanted to end filled the next hour or two of their night.

It took every ounce of willpower Keevah owned not to cry out in ecstasy when her release finally washed over her. Thrilling, intense, intoxicating. Lachlan's soon followed.

Any pain she'd felt before was gone. Something akin to bliss and joy came over her and she couldn't help but to cry. There were a hundred different things she wanted to tell him but didn't have the strength. Nay, she hadn't come to their marital bed an innocent blushing bride.

But the way he made love to her? 'Twas unlike anything she had ever experienced before. He wasn't there to slake his own desires. Nay, he was claiming her, letting her know with every touch, every kiss, every tender word that he loved her.

Worried he'd hurt her, Lachlan lifted his head and asked, "Are ye well? Did I hurt ye?"

Sobbing, she shook her head. "That was beautiful."

Feeling rather proud, he rolled onto his back, pulling her to lie beside him. She rested her head on his shoulder wrapping her arm around his chest and held him as if her life depended on it.

"I love ye, Keevah," he whispered as he caressed her arm and kissed the top of her head.

Swiping away her tears, she said, "I love ye, more than I ever thought possible."

THEY HAD SLEPT LIKE THE DEAD AND WOULD HAVE BEEN CONTENT to sleep longer had Brigid not wakened them early the next morn. "I am hungry," she told them. She was adorable with her tousled hair and sleepy eyes. "And I has to pee."

They all tended to their morning ablutions, dressed, and went below stairs to break their fast. Brigid, they soon learned, was, unlike her mother, very much an early bird. She happily chatted away as she ate her porridge and eggs. "Are there other children to play with?" she asked, referring to the new home they'd be heading to.

"Aye," Lachlan replied.

"Do ye think they will play with me?" she asked, shoving a big bite of porridge into her mouth.

He assured her they would, even though he wasn't certain yet exactly what he'd be going home to. Hopefully there hadn't been any further insurrections in his absence.

As they packed their belongings, he sent a silent prayer heavenward that Jamie and Fergus had been able to keep the peace. The image of them being attacked by the Chisolm clan bounced into his thoughts on more than one occasion.

Keevah hadn't brought much with her; in truth, she thought she'd only be in Inverness a day or two at most. Poor Brigid had even fewer belongings. Packing took very little time at all.

They walked out of the inn into the bright winter morning. Lachlan's men had readied the horses that brought them here. They had also purchased a very mild-mannered mare for Keevah to ride. Brigid insisted on riding with Lachlan.

Down the cobblestone streets of Inverness, they rode. 'Twas difficult to tell who was most relieved or excited to be away from the city. In the end, it didn't matter.

They had ridden for nearly two hours before Brigid asked a most poignant question. "Are there bad men where we are goin'?"

"Nay, lass," he told her. Could his answer be considered a lie? Honest to God he truly didn't know what they'd be returning home to.

"Because ye sent them all to Hell?"

Lachlan chuckled. "Aye lass."

"Good," she smiled up at him. "I dunnae like bad men."

"Neither do I, lass. Neither do I."

'TWAS AFTER NOONIN' TIME THE FOLLOWING DAY BEFORE THEY reached the gates of their new home. Lachlan was relieved to see it was still standing and that it was MacCullough and MacDougall men manning the walls.

Brigid's eyes grew wide in amazement, the same expression her mother bore. "It is huge!" Brigid proclaimed. "It is beautiful!"

Lachlan agreed with the former, but not the latter. For now, he'd reserve his opinion on the place until after he received his reports from Jamie and Fergus.

The men on the wall called out their greetings and soon the gates were being opened. Lachlan handed Brigid off to Keevah before leading them through. He kept his hand on the hilt of his sword, just in case.

The courtyard was filled with people. Wholly unlike the first time he had arrived. Children ran and played, women stood in huddled groups chatting away.

As soon as they saw Lachlan approach, they all raced toward him. "Welcome back, Laird!" they began to call out.

For a brief moment, he wasn't certain if he'd suffered an injury to his head and was now hallucinating.

They followed them into the inner bailey where stable boys rushed out to take their horses. Lachlan dismounted; a look of utter confusion etched on his face. He helped Brigid down first and handed her to one of his men.

After helping Keevah dismount, he kept her protectively close to his side. Sensing his unease, Keevah said, "What is the matter?"

He shook his head. "I am nae certain. They are all bein' … nice."

From the look she gave him, she thought him daft. He hadn't taken the time to warn her about the Chisolms. Of course, there hadn't been much time these past days, what with a madman killin' women and all that.

Looking around the bailey, his eyes lit on something highly unusual. A very auld looking man who was missing a leg.

Jamie and Fergus came bounding down the stairs and greeted him with broad smiles and slaps on the back.

"What the bloody hell is goin' on?" Lachlan exclaimed in a whisper.

"Well, it seems yer stance on sendin' people away for no good reason, had a profound impact on the clan's opinion of ye."

Incredulous, all he could do was stand with mouth agape. "Ye have got to be jestin'."

A wry grin came to Jamie's face. "Nay, Laird MacCullough, I dunnae jest."

"Many of those who had been sent away have returned. There are a few, however, who rather liked livin' in the forest. Either way, the people are truly happy."

Lachlan's attention was pulled away when he saw Murdoch running across the bailey. A very comely woman, with hair graying at her temples was rushing towards him. "Mum!" Murdoch called out as he scooped the woman up and twirled her around.

"I cannae believe my own eyes," Lachlan said with a shake of his head. "I just cannae believe it."

Brigid had squirmed her way out of the warrior's arms and ran to

Lachlan's side. She slipped her hand into his and stared inquisitively at Jamie and Fergus.

"What have we here?" Jamie asked.

"This is my daughter, Brigid."

The two men were stunned. "I dinnae ken ye had a daughter," Fergus said.

Lachlan smiled. "She came with my bride." Gently, he pulled Keevah to his side and smiled at his friends.

Once they got over the shock of what Lachlan had told them, they bowed at their waists and greeted her. "Welcome, m'lady."

As they were heading towards the keep, Murdoch approached with his mother in tow. "Laird! Laird!" he called out.

Their procession came to a halt as a very happy Murdoch Chisolm introduced his mother. "This is me mum, Elsbeth. Mum, this is our new laird, Lachlan MacCullough."

She smiled warmly and curtsied. "'Tis a pleasure, laird, a true pleasure."

"I ken ye want to be gettin' yer wife settled," Murdoch began. "But there is somethin' important we need to do first."

Curious, Lachlan crossed his arms over his chest. "And what might that be?"

Murdoch withdrew his sword. Jamie and Fergus were upon him in an instant. Murdoch laughed and struggled against their tight hold. "I am only meanin' to offer my fealty, ye dirty buggers."

Lachlan gave a curt nod to his men and ordered them to release Murdoch. Murdoch shrugged himself out of their grip and smiled. Firmly, he thrust his sword into the earth at Lachlan's feet. He knelt on one knee and bowed his head. "I, Murdoch Chisolm, hereby swear my fealty to ye, Lachlan MacCullough. As long as there is breath in my body, ye have my loyalty and my arm."

In a matter of moments, more Chisolms were surrounding Lachlan and swearing their fealty to him.

Sensing his abject confusion, Fergus leaned in and whispered, "Give them yer thanks, laird. We shall explain everythin' else to ye later."

Looking at the rapidly filling bailey, Lachlan's heart swelled with pride and a good measure of relief. He raised his arm high and shouted, "Unity for us! Unity for Scotland!"

The crowd erupted into cheers, hands waving high, repeating the chant, "Unity for us! Unity for Scotland!"

THAT NIGHT, THEY FEASTED ON ROAST GOOSE, PHEASANT, AND venison. Platter after platter of succulents, vegetables, and sweets were brought to the high table.

Lachlan sat on the bench with his men. He still refused to sit in the previous laird's chair. He also made it known he had no desire for a new one. He preferred to be seen as an equal to his men.

Keevah and Brigid sat to his left, Jamie and Fergus to his right. They ate and drank fine wine and copious amounts of ale without the worry of being poisoned.

This was not the same clan he had left behind.

Musicians played near the hearth as the gathering room was filled near to bursting with clanspeople. Those who hadn't been in the bailey upon his arrival, now filed in. A long line had formed and one by one, these people who a week ago despised and loathed him, were now giving him their fealty.

It hadn't taken might or strength to gain their loyalty or trust. Nay, this was fealty born from their hearts. Hearts that had missed those family members who had been sent away over the years. Hearts filled with a renewed sense of hope for their future. Gone now was the fear of being imperfect or ill or injured. Those days were long gone.

"Honest to God, I dinnae believe the place would still be standin'," Lachlan admitted to Jamie and Fergus. "I feared I would come back to an insurrection or rubble."

Jamie downed his ale and let out a loud belch. "I must admit, there were many times I thought the same. But as soon as ye made the proclamation that all were welcome that no one else would be sent away, everything changed."

Fergus nodded with a mouthful of venison. "The verra next day, people began goin' to the forest in search of their family members who'd been sent away. Word spread like fire, and before we kent it, more and more people were comin' back."

Keevah had been listening intently. "I cannae believe their old laird would do such a thing."

"'Twas a surprise to all of us," Lachlan said.

"I am glad ye put a stop to it," she said, smiling proudly at him. "Ye are a fine laird, MacCullough."

Lachlan looked out at the crowded room. Oh, how his life had changed these past few months.

Behind him was his past; a life filled with heartache and sorrow and loneliness.

Beside him sat the love of his life and her daughter. His heart swelled with joy and pride. God had certainly blessed him, more than he thought he deserved.

Ahead of him was a bright future, one he had never dared dream of. Hope. Hope for a prosperous clan. Hope for a united Scotland.

His quiet reverie was broken by Brigid tugging on his sleeve. She kept tugging until he leaned over to listen. "I has to pee."

Epilogue

E wan MacHolmes sat in his semi-dark room staring at the figure on the bed. The healer he had hired had worked for days to keep the man from dying. There were many moments when he was certain the man had succumbed to his injuries, only to be surprised long moments later by his rapid breaths.

The ravages of his injuries, the loss of blood, and the subsequent ravaging fevers had left him almost unrecognizable. Gaunt with sunken eyes, dry, gray skin... he'd lost so much weight he rather resembled a skeleton covered in skin.

The healer had left that morn, his pocket filled with Ewan's silver. "There is nothin' else I can do," he had told him.

"Just remember to keep yer mouth closed."

Now, twas the middle of the night and the man still clung to life.

Ewan had a thousand questions he needed to ask him. Something deep within needed answers. *Why? What possessed ye to do such a thing? What were ye thinkin'? How did ye come to this?*

The man coughed, softly at first, but soon, his body racked, the bed shaking as the rattling in his chest increased. Ewan held his head as he held a cup to his lips. "Drink."

There was no warmth to his voice. Up until the moment he discovered the truth about him, Ewan would have given his life for the sick and dying man. But now? The only reason he wanted him alive was so that he could ask all those burning questions racing in his mind and heart.

The cough quieted and for the first time in days, the madman opened his eyes. He squinted in the darkness, his eyes glassy and unfocused.

For a long, long moment the two men stared at one another. Ewan's eyes were filled with pain and contempt. His foe's? Soulless dark eyes glowered at him.

After an interminable time, the man took in a deep breath and smiled. 'Twas not the smile Ewan remembered from his youth. Nay, this was a malevolent, hateful smile. "Brother."

BookBub

Do you love books? Love getting great deals on books? Follow Suzan at BookBub and you will be notified whenever she has a new release or a special deal!

Also by Suzan Tisdale

<u>The Clan MacDougall Series</u>

Laiden's Daughter

Findley's Lass

Wee William's Woman

McKenna's Honor

The Clan MacDougall Boxed Set

<u>The Clan Graham Series</u>

Rowan's Lady

Frederick's Queen

<u>The Mackintoshes and McLarens Series</u>

Ian's Rose

The Bowie Bride

Rodrick the Bold

Brogan's Promise

<u>The MacCulloughs</u>

Black Richard's Heart

Lachlan's Heart

<u>The Clan McDunnah Series</u>

A Murmur of Providence

A Whisper of Fate

A Breath of Promise

The Clan McDunnah Boxed Set

<u>Moirra's Heart Series</u>

Stealing Moirra's Heart

Saving Moirra's Heart

Stand Alone Novels

Isle of the Blessed

Forever Her Champion

The Edge of Forever

In the Echo of a Kiss

The MacAllens and Randalls Series:

Secrets of the Heart

The Daughters of Moirra Dundotter Series:

Mariote

Esa

Muriale

Orabilis

The Brides of the Clan MacDougall

(A Sweet Series)

Aishlinn

Maggy

Nora

About the Author

USA Today Bestselling Author, storyteller and cheeky wench, SUZAN TISDALE lives in the Midwest with her verra handsome carpenter husband. All but one of her children have left the nest. Her pets consist of dust bunnies and a dozen poodle-sized, backyard-dwelling groundhogs – all of which run as free and unrestrained as the voices in her head. And she doesn't own a single pair of yoga pants, much to the shock and horror of her fellow authors. She prefers to write in her pajamas.

Suzan writes Scottish historical romance/fiction, with honorable and perfectly imperfect heroes and strong, feisty heroines. And bad guys she kills off in delightfully wicked ways.

She published her first novel, Laiden's Daughter, in December, 2011, as a gift for her mother. That one book started a journey which has led to more than twenty published titles. To date, she has sold more than 650,000 copies of her books around the world. They have been translated into Italian, French, German, and Spanish.

You will find her books in digital, paperback, and audiobook formats.

If you'd like to know more about upcoming releases you can sign up for email notifications at: https://www.suzantisdale.com/newsletter

www.ingramcontent.com/pod-product-compliance
Lightning Source LLC
Chambersburg PA
CBHW010556170726
48285CB00011B/2942